D0228406

A MESSAGE FROM CHICKEN HOUSE

I love cooking – actually, it's often more fun than eating what I make (or maybe that's just me)! All that chopping, mixing, seasoning and tasting – there's nothing better than getting together with friends and family to make a glorious concoction for us all to enjoy. And that's what Laurel Remington's delicious tale is all about: our downtrodden heroine gradually discovers the perfect ingredients for friendship and family – through cooking! Laurel certainly knows the recipe for a great story – and our own 'writers' bake-off judges at the *Times*/ Chicken House Children's Fiction Competition agreed, as they made this yummy novel the winner . . .

Bon appétit!

BARRY CUNNINGHAM
Publisher
Chicken House

THE SECRET COOKING CLUB

LAUREL REMINGTON

Chicken House

2 Palmer Street, Frome, Somerset BA11 1DS
chickenhousebooks.com

First published in Great Britain in 2016
Chicken House
2 Palmer Street
Frome, Somerset BA11 1DS
United Kingdom
www.chickenhousebooks.com

Cover and interior design by Helen Crawford-White
Typeset by Dorchester Typesetting Group Ltd
Printed and bound in Great Britain by CPI Group (UK) Ltd, Croydon CR0 4YY

The paper used in this Chicken House book is made from wood grown in sustainable forests.

3 5 7 9 10 8 6 4

British Library Cataloguing in Publication data available.

PB ISBN 978-1-910655-24-5
eISBN 978-1-910655-61-0

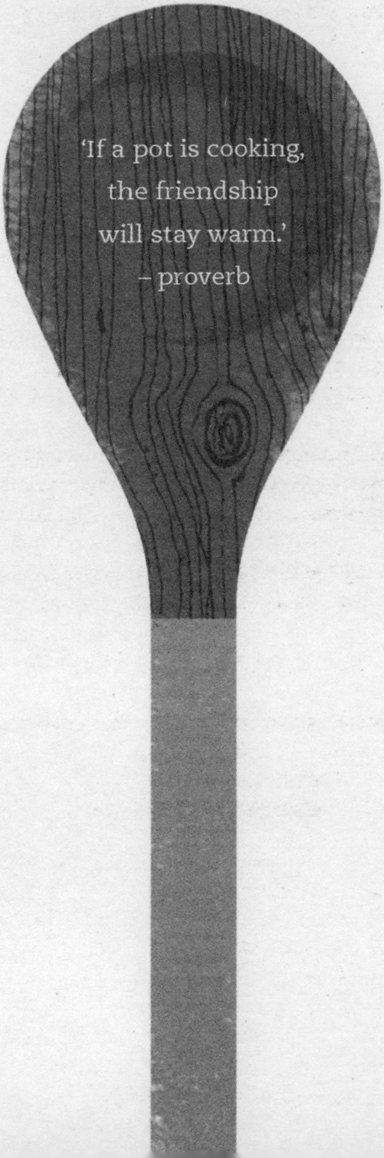

'If a pot is cooking,
the friendship
will stay warm.'
– proverb

1

THE WORST DAY OF THE WEEK

The ketchup bottle farts and the last dregs splutter on to my sister's toast. My stomach twists, but to be honest, I was already feeling sick. It's Friday morning, 7:50 a.m.

Ten minutes to go.

'Is there any more, Scarlett?' Kelsie wipes her chin with the sleeve of her school shirt, leaving a sticky red streak on the cuff.

'No,' I say. 'We're all out and Mum forgot to order more. But you've got enough.' I point to the lake of goop that's already smeared all over the toast – on top of the butter. Disgusting. Kelsie's almost seven, but she still eats everything with ketchup like it's some kind of fifth food group.

I push my soggy Weetabix around the bowl with the spoon, but I can't eat. My classmates are probably bouncing off walls now that it's almost the weekend; texting their friends; packing for sleepovers; making cool plans. But not me. Right now, I wish a hole would open up in the centre of our kitchen and swallow me up.

Because at 8:00 a.m. Mum's blog post goes live.

My eyes dart frantically around the kitchen. Maybe I could stop it by shutting off the power, or 'accidentally' dropping Mum's laptop in the bath, or becoming an amazing hacker and starting a virus that targets the computers of her thousands of followers – all in the next seven minutes. But I know it's too late. The new post is already on the server, hovering in cyberspace. Ready to pop into existence and broadcast the embarrassing details of my life to the world.

What will it be this week? I think back to everything I've done. Not much, since I quit all my clubs and activities at the end of last term. That put a stop to the posts about *Top ten reasons to bin your kid's violin*, and *Tap-dancing . . . did I give birth to three left feet?*

But even so, there's all the things I haven't done – like keeping my room tidy and making sure

Kelsie washes her hands after she uses the toilet. Two weeks ago, Mum did a 'funny' little quiz about it: *Which has more germs – my daughter's room or a public loo?* That one generated over two hundred comments from her followers, and got her five new advertisers for cleaning products on the site. That night, she ordered in a pizza so we could 'celebrate'. Kelsie ate my share (with ketchup) and I sat in my room wondering if it's ever going to end.

I give up on breakfast and take my bowl to the sink. The water runs upstairs and I can hear Mum humming. She stayed up late putting the finishing touches on her post, and the fact that she's up early must mean it packs a punch. 'Hurry up,' I say to Kelsie. 'I don't want to be late.' Not that I ever want to show my face at school again, but better that than see Mum and pretend we're some kind of normal family.

'But I *need* more ketchup.' Kelsie pouts down at her plate. She scrapes her soggy bread and licks the ketchup off the knife.

'Look, I'll get some at the shop after school, OK? Now go and put your shoes on.'

I grab her plate and take it to the bin. On top of the overflowing rubbish are a few pieces of balled-up paper. I fish one out and uncrumple it. It's a printout of Mum's new post that went live – I check my watch – one minute ago. I look at the title: *Bye-bye, Oxford, my daughter has no interests.*

The words blur on the page as my eyes swim with tears.

THE NEW GIRL

I walk Kelsie to the gate of her school. A few of the mums whisper to each other when they see me. They've all read the new post. When I walk up the hill to my school, a boy from the rugby team pulls a face at me. 'Bye-bye, Oxford.' He fakes a sob and a little wave. The two boys he's walking with start laughing. 'Hey, tell your mum we want another post about your knickers,' one of them shouts.

'How about one on *your* knickers,' I say, rolling my eyes. Because what else can I do other than play along? The day the post went up about the fact I still wore Disney Princess knickers was literally the most embarrassing of my life. Until the post *Did something die in that PE bag?* went up. And the one on our talk about the 'birds and the bees'. My face is burning as I hurry off to the classroom. I know that everyone at school has already read the latest post. There's nowhere to hide.

My first class is English. I take a seat at a table at the back, too flustered to realize that Gretchen is sitting right in front of me. She turns halfway round in her seat.

'Hi, Scarlett, you OK?' She sounds friendly, but I know it's all an act. Gretchen was one of the first girls to try to become 'new best friends' with me when Mum's blog got popular. Back then, I'd thought it was cool that so many people wanted to be my NBF. But then I overheard Gretchen and Alison whispering together. Gretchen was saying how she wished her mum would write a blog about her. It would be *so* much more interesting than my mum's blog because she was running for student PTA rep, whereas I was the 'most boring girl in the world'. I'd cleared my throat so she'd known I was there. 'Oh hi, Scarlett!' – she'd recovered like the PTA princess she is. 'How was your weekend?'

'Fine,' I'd said then, and now I just shrug and say nothing. I don't ask how she is, because (a) I don't care, and (b) I don't want to hear about the student council, her new lavender bedroom suite, her horse-riding lessons, or any of the other things that Gretchen does, because there's no one broadcasting her bad bits to the world.

Alison doesn't even bother to be friendly. She ignores me, rummaging in her bag for her lip gloss. Alison's beautiful – tall and blonde with perfect skin and big green eyes – and what's more, she knows it. If she was Mum's daughter, there would be no bad bits to broadcast. If I was her, I wouldn't have the time of day for people like me either.

Our form teacher, Ms Carver, comes into the room and starts writing on the whiteboard. The bell rings, and just then someone runs past me up the aisle to an empty seat at the front of the room. It's Nick Farr, the cutest boy in the whole world. All the girls in my year think so.

'Good of you to join us, Mr Farr,' Ms Carver says, raising her eyebrows.

'My pleasure,' Nick replies. He turns round in his seat and winks at Alison. My insides droop like a wilting flower. Not that I want a boyfriend yet or anything, but never in a million years will boys like Nick notice that I even exist. And under the circumstances, that's probably a good thing. I'd die if anyone found out I liked him and it ended up in Mum's blog.

Because that's another thing I have to thank Gretchen for. I ignored the 'most boring girl in the world' thing, and for a while, set about trying to make her like me. I worked on her PTA rep campaign, joined a few of the clubs she was in, helped her with her grammar homework, and tried really hard to be her friend.

But around then, Mum started blogging about more personal stuff – like that I bought a deodorant with my pocket money, that I still sleep with my old teddy, and that I was 'trying to get in with the popular crowd'. Things I'd never told Mum, because I'd stopped talking to her by then. Someone was leaking stuff. I had my suspicions, so I told Gretchen some made-up things – just stupid stuff about wanting to dye my hair pink and get my nose pierced. Some of it showed up in Mum's blog. I was mortified – but not very surprised. I confronted Mum but she managed to twist things around. She said that 'one of my friends was worried about me, and if I ever needed to talk she was there to listen . . .' blah, blah, blah (and that maybe when I turned thirteen next year I could get my ears pierced). Whatever. So that's when I quit all the clubs and activities, and stopped hanging out with Gretchen and Alison. I mean, why bother?

Ms Carver begins the lesson. My mind churns with thoughts about Mum, and how I wish that I could start a new life in a new town where no one knows me. Then maybe I could go back to being like I was before – a fun girl with lots of friends, eager to try new things, and laugh at myself when I made mistakes. Was I really that girl only a little over two years ago? I can barely remember a time when I didn't have this gnawing shame in the pit of my stomach.

I stare straight ahead at the clock on the wall, when all of a sudden I'm jarred back to reality by something Ms Carver is saying: '. . . and really, it takes a lot more than good marks to get into a top university.' I swallow hard. Of course – my teacher's read it too.

Just then, the door to the classroom opens. Mrs Franklin, the head teacher, walks in, followed by a girl I haven't seen before. She's wearing the same boring old uniform as the rest of us, but there's something about her that makes me look twice. For one thing, she's really pretty – with black, shiny hair, a roundish face and bow-shaped lips that seem to naturally curve into a smile. But more than that, she looks like she might be nice. She glances at me for a second and our eyes meet.

'Sorry to interrupt,' Mrs Franklin says. 'This is Violet Sanders. She's new today and she'll be joining you.'

The head teacher gestures to the one empty seat – two away from mine – and the girl sits down. She takes out a notebook and pencil from her bag, biting her lip like she's a little nervous.

'Fine. Welcome, Violet.' Ms Carver shuffles her papers and goes back to the lesson.

The new girl stares straight ahead. I glance over at her. *Violet*. I feel like we've got something in common because our names are both colours. But whereas my name seems all wrong – Scarlett is a name for a vibrant, sexy, confident girl; not one with dishwater blonde hair, a body that's all elbows and knees, and who'd rather hide in a bag than draw attention to herself – Violet's name seems to suit her. Even her eyes seem to be a bluish-purply colour. It crosses my mind that maybe we might be friends – if she doesn't know who I am, it would be like a clean slate. But just then, Gretchen looks at Violet over her shoulder and smiles. The breath fizzles out of my chest. That's it, then – Violet will be claimed by the popular crowd, my secret will be revealed, and that will be that.

And that's exactly what happens. After class, Gretchen and Alison walk Violet out of the room shoulder to shoulder like they've been best friends for ever. They eat lunch at the same table in the canteen. I watch them from across the room. Gretchen shows her something on her phone, and points at me. Violet glances over and I look away. Nick comes up to their table and sits down and they all start chatting and laughing together.

At that point, I can't take it any more. I get up, throw the remains of my tasteless beans and mystery-meat sausages in the bin, and hang about in the loos until the next class begins.

3

A BAD DAY FOR SOMEBODY

By the end of the day, everyone at school has lost interest in the blog post, and I'm off the hook for another week. I walk home slowly, too exhausted to be embarrassed any more. When I see Mum, I'll pretend that everything's fine – because if I don't, she'll just blog about my 'attitude', and how I don't appreciate the difficulties she faces.

Which is just so wrong. I kick hard at a rock in my path. I'm proud of Mum and what she's achieved. In less than three years, she's well on her way to becoming a really successful 'mummy blogger'. Each week, her followers log in to read her posts about the trials and tribulations of raising two children as a single mother after her husband ran off with his personal trainer. We rarely ever see Dad nowadays, and Mum refused to take any money off him from the moment he left – not even for me and Kelsie. She got on with her blog in order to support us. Which she's done.

Her proudest moment, at least as far as her followers are concerned, was when Dad came limping back a year or so ago, asking for a share of her blog money. She told him where to go in a vlog that went viral.

Now she writes her weekly post, and in between, she has a lot of guest bloggers posting to her site, and a 'Rant Page' for anyone to post on if they want to complain about their kids, husbands or partners, friends, work, mother-in-laws – whatever. She's got lots of advertisers, and is even working on a deal with Boots to make a 'Mum's Survival Kit' that they'll sell in all their stores.

So it's cool that she's an online celebrity, and while we're not rich or anything, she's made enough money for us to move into a three-bedroom house where I get my own room and don't have to share with my sister. But there's one big problem. Her trials and tribulations, rants and things she has to 'survive' mostly involve me, and sometimes Kelsie. I know she loves us, but sometimes I think she really must hate being a mum.

I walk slower and slower the closer I get to home. The thought of another evening spent watching *Tracy Beaker* with Kelsie makes me feel like a rag doll with the stuffing knocked out. I wonder what Violet is doing tonight. Probably spending a nice evening with her parents; telling them about her first day at school and the 'cool' new friends she's made; then settling down to play a board game, or practise piano, or learn Chinese or something—

As I turn down my road, my heart leaps to my throat. An ambulance with flashing lights is parked at the end of the terrace, right in front of our house. Two paramedics are loading a stretcher inside. Mum once told me that 'it's a bad day for somebody' whenever there's an ambulance, or the police come round.

I start to run, my school bag banging up and down on my back. Is it Mum? Kelsie? As the blue and white lights wink on and off, all the mean thoughts I've ever had about them flash before my eyes. I wish I could unthink them.

The paramedic shuts the ambulance door. I realize that they're actually in front of the house next door. An old woman called Mrs Simpson lives there. I've never met her, and I only know her name because a delivery man who was looking for her house came to ours by mistake. Her house is kind of spooky – the curtains are always closed and I've never seen a light on. When we moved here a few months ago, Mum talked about inviting her over for tea, but surprise, surprise, it never happened.

I walk up to the paramedic. 'Is Mrs Simpson OK?'

'She'll be fine. She had a bit of a fall,' he says. 'Got a bang on the head. She managed to dial 999, otherwise . . .' He shakes his head. 'You a relative?'

'No. I don't really know her.'

He climbs into the passenger seat. 'OK, well – she's in good hands now; we'll take it from here.'

The ambulance pulls away and the siren begins to wail. I stand alone on the pavement, watching until it disappears round the corner. In the other houses in the road, there's not even a curtain twitching in a downstairs window. No one seems to have noticed anything.

Inside our house, Kelsie's watching TV in the living room. I plunk down my bag and go to the kitchen. The door to Mum's office – the 'Mum Cave' – is open.

'Scarlett? Is that you?' she calls out.

'Yeah,' I say. Anger simmers in my chest. Mum has so many thousands of online 'friends', but has never paid the slightest bit of attention to the old lady next door. Not that I have either. And now it might be too late.

'Guess what?' Mum rushes out of her office like a slightly rumpled whirlwind. She enfolds me in a hug. For a second I almost give in to the comforting feeling and hug her back. But all too soon, the other stuff comes rushing back. I pull away.

'What?' I say warily.

'I'm in Boots! They signed the contract today. They're going to stock the survival kit in two hundred stores to start with. Isn't that brilliant?'

'Um, yeah.'

'Here, let me show you the prototype.' She goes to the counter and picks up a little box printed with purple and pink camouflage. 'We've got some hand lotion and sanitizer, a gel face mask, earplugs, lip balm, jellybeans, and a hollow chocolate egg with a *Mum's Survival Tip* inside.'

'Oh.'

'They wouldn't let me include the caffeine pills, but we're going to add a coffee sachet. You know, like a tea bag?'

'Great. Didn't you hear the ambulance?'

'What ambulance? Anyway, I've still got to choose the jellybean colours. What do you think about pink?'

'Pink's good.' Or *Scarlett* . . . I don't add.

'Brilliant. Pink it is. I'll email them now.' She

starts for the door of her office.

'Mrs Simpson had a fall,' I say. 'They took her to hospital.'

'Who?' She barely pauses.

'The neighbour next door. The old lady.'

'Oh, is that her name?'

'Yeah.'

'Well . . . too bad.' She gives a little shrug. 'Oh, and Scarlett, would you mind getting Kelsie her tea? I've got to prepare for tonight's online chat. It's on "how to talk to your teenager".'

'Sure,' I say through my teeth.

'Thanks. Oh, and Scarlett . . .'

'Yeah?'

'Thanks for being such a big help.'

She closes the door and I stare for a moment at the 'Mum Cave' sign swinging on its hook. Part of me wants to fling open the door and demand that she 'talk to her teenager' for real. I'd tell her exactly how I feel, tell her exactly how bad my day has been thanks to her, and tell her exactly where she, her two hundred Boots stores, and her thousands of online followers can go. But to be honest, it's just not worth it. Much better just to tick off my tasks one by one – dinner, homework, watching TV, shower – and just go to bed.

And that's exactly what I do. By the end of the evening, my anger has dulled and I start to feel numb. I collapse on to my bed more tired from doing nothing than if I'd run a marathon. And then I can't sleep. I think about Mrs Simpson. It's been a bad day for her – much worse than for me. I hope she's OK. I close my eyes and try to think good thoughts for her, but my mind keeps wandering. And then, just as I'm finally starting to drift off, I'm jolted awake again by an ear-splitting screech.

4

A NOISE IN THE NIGHT

I sit bolt upright in the circle of light from my lamp. That sound: it was like someone – or something – being tortured. And it came from the other side of the wall that separates our house from Mrs Simpson's. Panic floods through me. She must have come home from hospital and hurt herself again. Maybe this time she won't be able to get to the phone. Maybe this time she'll die and it will be my fault. And the headline of OLD WOMAN LEFT TO DIE AS GIRL IGNORES CRY FOR HELP will be in all the newspapers, not just on Mum's blog.

I swing out of bed and tiptoe into the hallway. My sister's room is dark and I can hear her breathing. There's a crack of light below Mum's door and the sound of typing. For a second I think of knocking. But she'll just tell me it's nothing and send me back to bed.

I sneak downstairs to the kitchen and grab a torch from the drawer by the sink. The door to the garden squeaks when I open it and, holding my breath, step outside. The moon is a perfect crescent and there are one or two stars twinkling among wispy clouds. I stand up on a bucket and peer over the fence. Nothing seems out of the ordinary. The back of Mrs Simpson's house is dark.

I go back into our house, tiptoe through the downstairs and out of the front door. Everything is silent in the road. A thin coat of dew has formed on the windscreens of the cars, the tiny droplets glittering in the moonlight. I go round the hedge that separates our house from Mrs Simpson's. Her door is black and glossy with a brass letter box and knocker. As I lift my hand to knock I hear it again – the bone-chilling wail from inside.

I forget all about knocking and wrench on the door handle. But it's locked. My heart thunders as I flip on the torch. There's an old flowerpot next to the door, and I check underneath it. Nothing. I look under the recycling bin and, finally, under the mat. A gold key glints in the circle of light. I mean – who actually leaves their key under the mat? I fumble with the key in the lock and push open the door.

The house is dark and silent, and smells of dusty curtains and Imperial Leather soap. I flick the torch around the room, scared that I might see a body lying in a pool of blood. Instead, there's some dark clunky furniture, a saggy three-piece suite, and lots of knick-knacks. The room says 'old lady'. I shine the torch towards the door at the back of the room that must lead to the kitchen, and all of a sudden I'm the one who yelps.

Eyes. Yellow and unfriendly. I'm so jumpy that it takes me a second to realize that it's not a monster or a ghost, but a cat – pure black, with a white collar around its neck.

'Oh, you scared me!' I say. And a second later, I realize how stupid I've been. 'It was you, wasn't it, making all that racket?'

The cat swishes its long, fluffy tail, still looking like some kind of demon in animal form. It takes a few steps towards me, holding its head haughtily in the air. My skin tickles as it rubs against my bare legs and starts to purr.

'You're lonely, is that it?' I reach down and pick up the cat. It nestles into my arms, staring at me with big eyes that now seem more sad than frightening. 'And hungry maybe?'

The cat rubs its cheek against mine.

I've never had a cat – or any kind of pet – but I

instinctively snuggle it closer in my arms like some kind of lost, kindred spirit.

'Those paramedics must have locked you out of the kitchen. Let's see if we can find you some food.'

The cat squirms in my arms and I put it down. It hurries over to a door that in our house leads to the dining room, and starts to meow. I open the door and switch on the light.

What I see makes me gasp.

5

ROSEMARY'S KITCHEN

The kitchen is amazing – that's the only word for it. It's vast – with a high, beamed ceiling and a spotless floor. Every surface sparkles: shiny stainless steel, polished wood, mirror-black granite. Copper pots hang from a rack on the ceiling, and there's an entire wall of cookbooks. In one corner is a giant cooker, next to a double-width fridge, and a glass cupboard filled with just about every kind of kitchen gadget. A wooden table takes up the entire back of the room, and there's a fireplace big enough to stand up in. The whole thing seems like heaven for a cook – and anyone around to eat the food. I breathe in the heady smell of spices and fresh lemon and realize that I'm smiling. I can't believe all this is here – just on the other side of the wall from the three rooms that make up our poky little kitchen, dining/junk room and the Mum Cave.

The cat meanders over to an empty bowl next to the cooker. It looks at me with its big yellow eyes and begins to meow. Venturing inside, I go over to the fridge. A magnetic sign on the door says 'Rosemary's Kitchen'. Inside, it's stocked with practically a whole supermarket's worth of fresh food. I take out a carton of organic milk and an open tin of tuna-flavoured cat food. 'I guess Mrs Simpson's name must be Rosemary,' I say, emptying the milk and cat food into bowls. 'I didn't know.'

The cat swishes its tail disdainfully, and dives into the food. I continue looking around. I'm immediately drawn to the shelves of cookbooks – one whole shelf is dedicated to a series of books called *Encyclopaedia of Herbs and Spices*. The shelf at eye level has three different cookbooks by Mrs Beeton, plus a few big-name celebrity cookbooks: Delia Smith, Jamie Oliver, Mary Berry – but most of them look almost new. There are some well-used books by authors I don't recognize, like Elizabeth David, Julia Child and Auguste Escoffier. But what interests me most is the top shelf. It has an assortment of very old-looking books in various colours, shapes and sizes. I grab one that catches my eye: *Recipes Passed Down from Mother to Daughter*. It's got a drawing of a pretty 1950s mum on the cover, giving her apple-cheeked daughter some biscuits fresh out of the oven. Somehow I'm pretty sure it won't have an entry for 'frozen fish fingers and chips' which is the only recipe that my mum's 'passed down' to me.

I put it back on the shelf. Behind me, the cat is purring and eating at the same time. I turn round and something on the kitchen worktop catches my eye. Propped open on a wooden bookstand is a notebook bound in tattered red cloth, the front marbled in red, green and blue. It must be really old. Curious to see what Mrs Simpson was cooking before her accident, I pick it up. The book feels oddly warm in my hands, like a fresh-baked loaf of bread. I open the cover. On the first page is a note; loopy letters handwritten in black ink:

To my Little Cook – may you find the secret ingredient.

I read the words aloud to the cat, wondering who the Little Cook was, and whether she – or he – found the secret ingredient. The cat swishes its tail, quite content with the food in its bowl.

I flip through the notebook. There are loads of recipes written out in pen, with a few notes and crossings-out, but there are also pictures – some done in pencil and crayon, others cut out of magazines and old newspapers and glued to the page – of cakes, pies, bread, meat and other foods. There's also a whole section of recipes based on nursery rhymes with little poems and stories like 'Hansel and Gretel' written out in fancy lettering. It must have taken so much time to collect and write out the recipes and all the little rhymes and illustrations – years maybe. How lucky the Little Cook must have been to have someone care so much. I don't know anything about cooking, but as I hold the recipe book in my hands, I have a funny feeling that the book is special somehow.

I close the notebook. The cat has finished its tuna and begins lapping up the milk like an after-dinner coffee. Then it carefully licks its whiskers. Swishing its tail, it walks haughtily out of the kitchen. I turn the light off and follow it to the front room. It leaps on to one of the threadbare chairs.

'You're welcome,' I say, somewhat huffily. 'And I guess you'll be expecting me to come back tomorrow to feed you again?'

The cat curls up into a ball, snuggling its face into its wispy black tail. Its purrs grow slower, and soon it's fast asleep.

I move silently to the front door and shut off the torch so that no one will see me. I slip out of Mrs Simpson's house, with the handwritten recipe book still tucked underneath my arm.

THE LITTLE RECIPE BOOK

I don't really know why I took the notebook from Mrs Simpson's kitchen. It's not like I'm actually going to *cook* anything at home. I can picture Mum rubbing her hands with glee if I did: *Help, my daughter is trying to poison me/burn down the house/make me throw up during my marketing meeting with Boots.* I stick the recipe book under my pillow. Part of the reason I keep my room – according to one of Mum's blog posts – 'like a toxic waste dump' is so that she won't ever go in there.

Downstairs the next morning, Mum is blustering around in the kitchen, taking two minutes out of her busy day to drink a cup of instant coffee.

'So do you have any plans for the weekend, Scarlett?' Mum says.

'Um . . .' My brain furiously calculates the probabilities of providing her with blog material, depending on whether I say 'yes' or 'no'. I settle on: 'Not really, but I've got some homework to do.'

'Kelsie's gone to a birthday party this morning and I've got a guest blog post to write. Can you go over to Stacie's house?'

'She's visiting her grandma,' I lie. Stacie was my best friend last year, before the whole Gretchen and Alison thing. Then Mum wrote a post called *Psst . . . want to know a secret? My daughter's best friend is really thick*. And then, big surprise – Stacie stopped speaking to me and dropped me as a friend. Luckily, she goes to a private school so I don't have to see her every day.

'That's nice.' Mum puts down the coffee cup and digs around in the fridge. She takes out a piece of cold pizza and nibbles on it. 'And how's school – you doing any new clubs?'

'No, Mum.' I take a box of cereal from the top of the fridge and pour some into a bowl. Then I sit down and stare at it.

Mum shakes her head and tsks. 'I just don't know what's up with you, Scarlett. When I was your age, I had lots of friends. Plus I did swimming and netball and . . .'

I stop listening. Mum's already written a soppy blog post called *I really was your age once . . .* where she went on about the days before mobile phones, iPads and Snapchat, when she and her friends passed notes in class and gossiped about boys. That post alone got over three hundred and fifty sympathetic comments from her followers. She won't write another one that's too similar, so I'm off the hook.

'Yeah, Mum, I know. But I'm sure Oxford University can live without me.' I force myself to take a bite of the cereal. It tastes like soggy cardboard.

Mum frowns. 'Well, if you're not doing anything, maybe you can pick up a few things for me at the shops.'

'Sure, whatever.' I take my bowl to the sink.

'You didn't eat any of that cereal.' Mum's eyes sharpen. 'Is something wrong?'

'No.' I pause for a second. 'I'm just not hungry.'

She cocks her head. 'You're not anorexic, are you?'

'No, Mum. It's just that the cereal's a little stale.'

'Oh.' She tosses the pizza crust in the rubbish and puts the kettle back on to boil. When she's not looking, I take the crust out of the bin and put it in the compost bucket instead.

'OK, Scarlett, whatever you say.' Mum glances

at me over her shoulder. 'But you're a growing girl – almost a real teenager. You need to keep your blood sugar up.' I can almost see the gears in her brain working overtime: *Idea for new blog post = is my daughter anorexic – or just obstinate?*

'Whatever, Mum. I'll have a snack later.'

I go up to my room and take out the little recipe book from underneath my pillow. I open it and reread the inscription inside the cover: *To my Little Cook – may you find the secret ingredient.*

I wonder what it was like for the Little Cook – a daughter or son, I assume – to spend time with their mum learning how to bake and cook wonderful things. One thing's for sure, I can't imagine *my* mum ever doing something like that with me.

I flip through the nursery rhyme section of the notebook, smiling at the recipes for pies, bread and gingerbread, and the little rhymes about 'The Cat and the Fiddle', and 'Goosey, Goosey Gander'. There are a few recipes for basic things: 'Humpty Dumpty's Perfect Eggs'; and 'Yankee Doodle's Four-cheese Macaroni'. There's also an 'ABC of Spices', most of which I've never heard of. But lots of the ingredients make my mouth water: buttercream, ginger, golden syrup, cocoa and caster sugar. Best of all are the cinnamon scones. There's a picture done in pen and coloured in with crayon of little fluffy triangles steaming hot in a basket with a red and white gingham cloth. My stomach rumbles just thinking about them. If I could try just one recipe, it would be that.

But I can't try any of the recipes. Not here at home where Mum would know about it.

So I'll have to find another way.

7

THE HOUSE NEXT DOOR

The street is quiet as I slip out of the front door. I walk up the weedy stone path to Mrs Simpson's house. I tell myself that it's not really breaking and entering when there's an old lady in the hospital and a cat that needs feeding. And a recipe book that needs returning. It's a no-brainer really. And if, by some chance, Mrs Simpson is already home from hospital, I'll tell her I came over to look after the cat.

No one answers when I knock on the door. The key is still under the mat. With a quick glance around to make sure no one's watching, I let myself into Mrs Simpson's house.

The first thing I see are those two yellow eyes again, shining like twin moons. The cat meows impatiently like it's been waiting for me and I'm late. 'Hi,' I say. 'You still here by yourself?' The cat swishes its tail. It gets to its feet and leads the way to the kitchen.

I get down to business – scoping out where everything is so that I can get on with my plan. Just being here again has made up my mind. I've found a special little recipe book and the perfect kitchen just on the other side of the wall. And now . . .

I'm going to cook something.

One by one I open the cupboards. It's like exploring a supermarket baking aisle. There are dozens of little jars and tins of herbs and spices. There are bags of flour: stoneground, buckwheat, spelt, malted wheatgrain; and sugars: demerara, caster, icing, muscovado – who knew there were so many different kinds? Even though everything is labelled, it's still kind of overwhelming. The cat rubs against my leg and stands in front of one of the cupboards.

'OK, OK, I get it. You're hungry again.' I open the cupboard and find a large supply of cat food. I dig around some more until I find a tin-opener in a drawer, along with a complete set of baking utensils and electric appliances, most of which I've no idea what to do with, and some of which look like scary dentist instruments.

Once the cat has its head contentedly in its bowl, I take out the little recipe book and set it on the bookstand. It practically falls open to the recipe for cinnamon scones. I read over the instructions: mixing everything together, then rolling out the dough and cutting out little triangle shapes that are to be dusted with more cinnamon and sugar. Then they're supposed to rise and become all fluffy in the oven. It sounds straight-forward enough, but suddenly I start to feel nervous.

What business do I have breaking and entering, and using Mrs Simpson's things? And worse, what makes me think that I can possibly bake anything? I've never really tried before, except once. I wanted to surprise Mum with a cake for her birthday so I bought a mix at the corner shop. It turned out that I didn't have enough eggs, and the butter was as hard as a rock. The mixture ended up all powdery and lumpy. Then I left it in the oven too long, and it came out charred and practically on fire. I threw it in the bin before Mum even knew I'd tried.

I take a deep breath – I'm here now so I may as well have a go. Most of the ingredients I need – flour, butter, baking powder, salt – are already set out on the worktop, along with a jar of Ceylon cinnamon. Strange that I didn't notice them last night. It's almost like Mrs Simpson had been getting ready to bake scones. It makes me feel a bit creepy – almost like she's here with me in the kitchen, looking over my shoulder, making sure I do it right. I peek quickly behind me. There's no one there.

'Silly,' I say aloud. Everything seems normal again. Finished eating, the cat curls up in its basket next to the cooker and begins licking its paws. I wash my hands and grab a rose-patterned apron from a hook by the fridge. Before I can lose my nerve, I put it over my head and tie it round my waist. *I'm ready*.

I've never been one of those kids who liked playing in sand, making mud pies, finger painting or generally making messes. So that might be why I'd never guessed how satisfying it could be to measure out ingredients that by themselves look like nothing, put them into a bowl, then stir them together. Peering out of its basket, the cat keeps an eye on my progress.

At first the mixture is lumpy and dry, and all my worries come back that I've done something wrong. I think about adding more milk, but I decide, just this once, to trust the recipe. I keep on stirring. The smell of cinnamon goes to my head, and for some reason I feel happier and calmer than I've been in ages. When the dough is a soft mass in the bowl, I sprinkle some flour on the worktop to start rolling it out.

But all of a sudden, disaster strikes. The doorbell rings, and a key turns in the lock.

A TASTE OF CINNAMON

Someone's here! Panicking, I look around. I could dash out of the back door, but I'd be trapped in the garden, and besides, the kitchen's a mess and it's obvious what I've been doing. The cat jumps up from its basket like it's trying to figure out how to cover for me. I pull off the apron and start trying to clean up – for all the good it's going to do. And then I hear a woman's voice: 'Look, I'm sorry if you're bored, but I have to do this. You said you wanted to come. Next time, stay at home.'

I don't hear a reply because the front door closes and something – a handbag maybe? – thunks to the floor. Then there's the sound of heels clicking in the hallway. I look around for a place to hide – the broom cupboard? The hearth? Inside the oven?

The knob on the door turns. I stand there paralysed, my heart thundering. The cat comes up beside me, the fur on its back standing up. The door opens. I come face to face with just about the last person I was expecting to see . . .

Violet.

'Oh, you scared me!' Her hands fly to her mouth. 'I . . . I didn't know anyone was here.'

'Um, yeah.' I smile through my teeth. 'I was just . . . just—'

'Violet? Is there someone in there?'

Frantically, I gesture at the cat.

'No, Aunt Hilda. Just a cat.' Violet gives a fake-sounding sneeze for effect.

'All right,' Aunt Hilda says. 'I'm going to start with the upstairs. Don't touch anything, OK?'

'OK.'

The high heels click up the stairs.

'Thanks for that,' I say. My heart slows to a fast jog.

'What are you doing here?' She eyes the kitchen and the mess I've made.

'I was making scones,' I say sheepishly. 'Cinnamon.'

She sniffs the air. 'It smells good in here. Not

cinnamon, though – but something else?'

'I don't know – butter maybe? Or the dough? But dough doesn't really smell like anything, does it?'

'It's nice.' She smiles. 'But you don't live here, right? My aunt said the house belongs to some old lady.'

'Mrs Simpson,' I say. 'Rosemary. She's a neighbour. We live next door.'

'Oh. It's cool that she lets you use her kitchen.'

'Yeah . . . it is.'

'Violet?' The aunt's voice comes from upstairs. 'Did you say something?'

'No, Aunt Hilda,' Violet calls out.

'OK, but I need to see the—'

The aunt appears at the kitchen door, the clicking of her heels coming to an abrupt stop. She's about Mum's age but much taller in her heels, and she has the same blue-black hair as Violet. She's wearing a neat grey suit and a floral scarf.

'. . . kitchen,' she trails off, her mouth gaping open. 'Wow,' she says, 'it's . . . big.' She glances around. 'What a fantastic space. And look at the range cooker – it's enormous.' She gestures towards the cast-iron cooker that's as big as a small car.

'It's huge,' I agree.

Her eyes come to rest on me. 'And who are you?'

'I'm Scarlett. From next door. I . . . uh, came over

to feed the cat.'

'Looks like you're feeding yourself too.' Frowning, she gestures at the mess of flour and dry ingredients sprinkled on the worktop and the floor. 'If you're here without permission, then you'd better be gone when Mr Kruffs arrives.'

'Mr Kruffs?' The name sounds vaguely familiar. 'Who's he?'

Violet's aunt sizes me up like she's debating whether to answer. 'Emory Kruffs. He's running for local MP.' She wanders over and examines the cooker. 'You may have seen his name on posters.'

'Maybe.'

'I'm an estate agent – and he's arranged for me to give him a valuation on the house. He's supposed to meet me here.'

'Is it his house?' I ask.

'Well,' she frowns. 'Not exactly. I think he's the nephew of the owner.'

'Rosemary Simpson,' I say. 'She's the lady who lives here. Do you know if she's OK?'

She shrugs. 'No idea, sorry.'

'Well, someone needs to feed the cat until she gets back,' I say firmly. 'I mean, I'm sure Mrs Simpson wouldn't want it to starve. And I live right next door.'

'The cat . . .' she muses. 'I see your point, but if Mr Kruffs sees this mess, then I don't know . . . I wouldn't let him catch you here—'

'I was just leaving,' I say. 'That is – after I cut out the scones and put them in the oven.' I wince. 'And, you know . . . um . . . take them out again. Is that OK?'

'Cool,' Violet says. 'Can I watch?' She looks doubtfully at her aunt.

Something beeps loudly, startling us all. A text message. Aunt Hilda takes out her BlackBerry and stares at the screen. 'This must be your lucky day,' she says. 'Mr Kruffs just cancelled our meeting.'

Violet and I look at each other and grin.

Aunt Hilda checks her watch. 'I'm going to finish looking around and draft the email for the valuation,' she says. 'You two had better make sure this kitchen is spotless when you're done.' Her heels click away to the front room where she switches on a table lamp.

I turn to Violet. 'Thanks for staying,' I say. 'I mean, it was kind of creepy being here by myself. Especially if that Mr Kruffs turns up.'

'No problem,' Violet says. 'It's not like I've got anything better to do. And I've always liked scones – that is, if you're sharing.' Her smile grows wider.

'I'll think about it,' I laugh. We both peer into the bowl of mixed-up dough. I breathe in deeply. It smells delicious and . . . doughy. I put the soft ball on the worktop and gently roll it out. The rolling pin sticks a little to the dough, so I sprinkle more flour over the ball, trying to look like I know what I'm doing.

'Did your mum teach you how to cook?' Violet sounds almost impressed.

'No.' My mind whirls, trying to think of something cool – like my grandma was a *Bake Off* finalist – or something. But I don't want to lie to Violet. I point to the recipe book. 'Actually, I've never done it before,' I say. 'I'm teaching myself.' Flustered, I turn away from her and concentrate on cutting the dough into little triangle shapes. I check the recipe again, and sprinkle a sweet-smelling mixture of cinnamon and sugar on the tops.

'No – you're having a laugh.' Violet giggles in amazement. 'You've done this before. Right?'

I stand up a little straighter. 'Yeah, I guess I have. I can make cheese on toast. Does that count?'

'Yes, it does! I can't even make toast without burning it.'

'Well, I can barely even plug in the toaster!'

We look at each other and both start laughing. It's not like it's really *that* funny, but I'm so out of practice that my side begins to hurt. I kind of get the idea that maybe it's the same for her.

Violet helps me cut out the rest of the scones and we put them on a buttered baking tray. As we work, I tell her about the ambulance taking Mrs Simpson away, and about the cat, and how I broke into the house and found the recipe book and the kitchen. 'I had no idea it was here,' I say. 'Right on the other side of the wall.'

'It's awesome,' Violet says. She picks up the recipe book and flips through it. 'And this book – I can't believe someone took the time to write all this out by hand.'

'Yeah,' I say. 'I wonder who the Little Cook was.'

Violet reads the inscription inside the cover. 'And the secret ingredient – what's that?'

'I don't know.'

She goes back to the page with the scone recipe. 'Well, I can see why you wanted to have a go at making these scones,' she says. 'They look so delicious.'

'Yeah.' My brow furrows in concentration. We've cut out all the scones and I can't put off any longer the thing I've been dreading: tackling the range cooker.

'Ever used one of these things before?' I ask futilely.

'I don't think I've ever even seen one.' We both bust up laughing again. She helps me carry the trays over.

I look inside one of the cast-iron doors. Luckily, there are some wire racks – it looks like a normal oven once you open the doors. ‘Look,’ Violet says, ‘there’s a temperature dial. What should I put it on?’

I put the trays down and check the recipe in the notebook. ‘Put it on 220 degrees.’ I decide not to spoil the moment by mentioning that we were supposed to preheat the oven. Oh well. ‘They should be ready in about twenty minutes.’

‘I can’t wait to try one,’ Violet says.

My stomach rumbles in agreement.

9

THE SCENT OF CHILDHOOD

When I get home, I'm surprised to see Mum sitting at the table helping Kelsie read her phonics book. 'Where have you been?' she asks me without looking up. 'No, Kels, there's an "l" – it's "pool", not "poo".'

'I went to the library to do some homework.'

'Oh.' She sounds disappointed. There's very little blogging material in me going to the library, but I'm sure that my sister's 'pool'/'poo' confusion will figure prominently in the next post. 'Well, next time let me know, OK?'

'OK.'

'And I hope you're hungry, because I made

baked macaroni cheese. It's on the hob.'

'Really?' I raise an eyebrow. Even though I'm stuffed to the gills with the most delicious, fluffy, puffy cinnamon scones I could ever imagine eating – let alone making myself – I feel kind of sorry that I missed what, in our house at least, passes for a real meal.

'I'll have a little,' I say. 'Sorry, I didn't know you were cooking.'

'I wasn't going to.' She leans forwards on her elbows. 'I mean, *me*? Cook?' she gives a little laugh. 'But it was the oddest thing . . .'

'What?'

'I was in my office, and all of a sudden there was this smell.' Her brow furrows. 'Some kind of spice – cinnamon, maybe. It reminded me of something. I don't know what really. Something from my childhood.'

'Your childhood?' I try not to sound surprised. One thing that Mum never talks or blogs about is her childhood, before she got to teenage years anyway. Sometimes I wonder if she was ever my age.

She shrugs. 'I guess a neighbour must have been cooking. All of a sudden, it was like I was back in my grandma's kitchen. They do say that smell is one of the strongest senses for triggering memories.' She stares at the cooker for a second.

'That's interesting,' I say. 'What was your grandma like? You never really talk about her.'

She blinks quickly. 'Oh, I don't know.' She waves away my question. 'I guess my nose is just extra sensitive today. You'd think I was pregnant or something.' She stands up and puts the kettle on, twisting her hands in what I recognize as her *I've just thought of something to blog about* way. 'I mean, when I had you girls in my tummy, I was throwing up left and right. For all nine months of it, each time. Everything tasted like salt and' – she laughs – 'seemed to smell like dog poo!'

'Mummy, you said poo!' Kelsie says triumphantly.

'Oops, I meant 'pool' of course!' Mum points back to the book and she and Kelsie both giggle. Even I have to smile, though we are all *far* too old for that kind of joke. I serve myself a small bowl of macaroni cheese, mulling over what Mum said about how she could smell the cooking through the wall. It's kind of odd that she's never mentioned it before. I mean, before her accident, Mrs Simpson must have cooked all the time.

I sit down at the table with the bowl and take a bite. I'm so surprised that I almost choke. 'It's *good*, Mum,' I say.

'I made the sauce myself.'

'You did?'

She narrows her eyes. 'Don't look so surprised. Believe it or not, Scarlett, not everything is made in the microwave.'

Later that night, as I'm lying on my bed staring at the glow-in-the-dark stars on my ceiling, I think about everything that's happened over the last two days – from the yowling cat, to the kitchen and cookbook – from meeting Violet unexpectedly, to Mum's home-made cheese sauce.

Most of all, though, I think about making the scones. My mouth waters as I remember their comforting doughy taste. Because I hadn't preheated the oven, we left them in for much longer than they should have needed. I was kind of stressed out that they would be burnt. But when we took them out, they were nice and golden brown on the bottom. To me, they tasted perfect.

They looked perfect too – Violet even snapped a few pics of them on her phone.

She and I each ate two, and Violet's aunt ate one. I wrapped the rest up and stored them in a plastic container – they're still downstairs in my bag, fourteen of them. I feel a little bit mean for not sharing them with Kelsie and Mum, but I don't want to explain where they came from.

When I hear Mum's bedroom door close, I tiptoe downstairs, unwrap the scones and leave two of them out on a plate on the kitchen table. Let Mum and her followers try to figure out who made them. She'll never guess in a million years that it was her boring old daughter. I climb back in my bed and drift off to sleep, still breathing in the phantom smell of cinnamon.

A DOLLOP OF TEARS

The next morning the scones are gone (with a plate of crumbs left behind on the table) and the door to the Mum Cave is shut.

The day goes slowly – the usual sort of Sunday: Mum working, me playing with Kelsie until Mum comes out and zaps dinner in the microwave, then falls asleep on the sofa . . . I creep into Mrs Simpson's house just before teatime to feed her cat, but I feel uneasy there by myself. What if her nephew comes round today after Violet's aunt talks to him? I sneak out again, wondering if I'll ever have the courage to go back there and use the kitchen. Or will the scones be our first and last attempt?

The next morning, Mum is up and in her office by the time I come downstairs. I can hear Mum's voice, talking animatedly to someone on her mobile. By the time I'm ready to leave for school, and have got Kelsie ready too, Mum still hasn't come out. I feel kind of sad that she hasn't even bothered to come out to say goodbye to us. But when I pick up my bag (filled with a dozen scones) and leave the house, I feel better.

As class is about to begin, Violet comes up to me in the hall. 'Do you have them?' she whispers behind her hand. I feel a little flicker of pride when I see that, behind her, Gretchen and Alison are looking in our direction.

'Yeah,' I say. 'I gave one – well, two, actually – to Mum. But I've got the rest with me. Do you want one?'

'Later.' Violet smiles conspiratorially. 'In fact, I have an idea.'

'What?'

'You'll see. Leave them with me. And come to the canteen at lunchtime, OK?'

I ignore a tiny stab of alarm. 'OK.'

Worry knots in my chest later on as I walk into the canteen. On a table at the centre is a large pink and purple Easter basket. I watch as a few kids go up to it and peer inside. There's a sign taped to the handle of the basket.

FREE SAMPLES!

My stomach clenches. I sit down at a table near the door and watch the steady stream of people going up to the basket and helping themselves. A moment later, Violet plunks down beside me.

'Do you like my surprise?' she whispers.

I stand up awkwardly. 'Um . . . I'll see you later, OK. I've got to see Ms Carver about an essay I wrote.'

Violet stops smiling. 'What's up with you?'

'Nothing.' My voice catches. 'You didn't tell anyone that I helped make the scones, did you?'

'No, I didn't. But what's the problem? Everybody loves them.'

I look over to the central table. People are hovering around like wasps at a picnic. Some kids are talking to other kids that I know for sure aren't their friends. The volume of chat in the room rises steadily. There were only twelve scones, but people seem to be sharing them out – even the crumbs.

'Yeah, great. It's just . . . could you not mention my name? I mean – can you say that you made them?'

Violet puts her hands on her hips. 'For your information, no one saw me put them there. I thought it would be fun to have it be a secret. I'm not going to say who made them.'

'Oh.' I feel so stupid. I can't tell Violet about why I don't want to be involved – it all just sounds so lame.

'So, what's wrong, Scarlett?'

'Nothing.' I turn away and leave the canteen.

I rush down the corridor. Violet could have been my friend and I've ruined it. Why can't I just tell her the truth – that I'm scared to do anything because of Mum and her stupid blog. Why did I go to Mrs Simpson's house, and why did Violet have to find me? Why did Violet have to come to our school at all?

In the girls' loos, I practically slam into Gretchen and Alison who are on their way out. 'Hey, watch it.' Gretchen teeters backwards.

I lock myself in a cubicle.

'You OK, Scarlett?' Gretchen almost manages to sound concerned.

'Come on, Gretch,' Alison says.

'I think she's crying.'

'No I'm not!'

'Whatever.'

I wait in the cubicle until I'm sure they're gone. A part of me knows that I'm acting totally irrational – like I'm outside my own body watching a crazy person. And then a new coldness washes over me. What if Gretchen tells Mum that she saw me crying like a big baby?

The loo door bangs behind me as I run out into the hall. Keeping my head bowed low, I push past the people in the corridor and run out of the school.

11

A SPOONFUL OF SECRETS

What am I doing? Where am I even going? I hurry past the shops, practically knocking down an old man pulling along a battered shopping trolley. I almost get hit as a lorry grinds to a stop in the middle of the zebra crossing. All the time I'm heading towards home – but I don't want to go home. Thoughts flash into my head: *Help! My selfish daughter tried to run away*, or worse: *Help! My daughter ran away and then, unfortunately, came back!*

Panting for breath, I finally stop. I'm standing on the doorstep of Mrs Simpson's house. I get the key out from under the mat, open the door and let myself inside.

The cat is there just inside the door. I scoop it up and sob into its black fur. It purrs in my arms but flicks its tail, like it's deciding whether or not to tolerate me.

'I'm sorry,' I say, setting it down. 'You've got your own problems, haven't you?'

The cat struts into the kitchen, meowing for food. I follow slowly behind, my heart finally slowing in the calm quiet of Mrs Simpson's kitchen. The recipe notebook is on the bookstand where I left it. But I'm almost positive that I left it open on the scones page. Now, it's flipped open to a page on 'Pat-a-cake Flapjacks'. There's a drawing cut from an old book and pasted on to the page of a little boy in a puffy white baker's hat. There's a hand-drawn border around him of steaming pies and iced cakes.

I flip through the notebook, my mouth watering at the possibilities: Hansel and Gretel's Gingerbread, Knave of Hearts Strawberry Tarts, The Princess and the Pea Soup, Simple Simon's Cottage Pie. But in the end, I turn back to the Pat-a-cake Flapjacks. Whatever they are – I need to make them.

Just like before, nearly every ingredient called for in the recipe is almost immediately to hand – like some kind of magic baking elf has been at work. Next to the recipe book, there are even two bars of Belgian cooking chocolate on the work-top that I swear weren't there last time. It's definitely a little weird, but I decide to make the best of it. I put on an apron, wash my hands and get started. I even remember to preheat the oven this time.

The cat sits and watches as I work. First, I read through the recipe so I know exactly what I'm doing. Then, I measure out the 'wet' ingredients – butter, golden syrup, a dollop of honey – into a pan. I add the brown sugar and cinnamon, and place the pan on the hob. I swirl the ingredients around with a wooden spoon over a low heat. The colours mix together – warm shades of brown and gold, marbled through with the bright yellow of the butter. The spicy scent goes straight to my head. It's fun watching all the separate parts of the mixture melt together like they've always belonged that way. When everything is uniform and liquid, I take the sticky mixture off the hob and mix in the porridge oats. The ingredients clump on the spoon. I scrape some off with my finger and taste it. It melts on my tongue, tasting wholesome and delicious.

I'm so caught up in what I'm doing that when the doorbell rings I practically jump out of my apron.

I'm not expecting to get lucky a second time. I'm sure it's Mr Kruffs, or maybe even the police. My heart starts to thud, but to be honest, what I'm most worried about is the syrup mixture getting cold before I can finish stirring in the oats.

I open the door. Standing there is the one person I didn't expect to see after the way I acted at school – Violet.

And I'm very glad to see her.

'Can I come in?' she says.

'Sure.' I stand aside and she comes inside the house. She sets down her school bag, and next to it, the empty Easter basket.

'Everyone loved the scones,' she says. 'That cinnamon – it really packed a punch. And it was even better because no one could work out who made them.'

'That's good.' I nod uneasily. It's just so weird that the whole school was talking about the scones that I made – which is the last thing I wanted. I turn and she follows me through to the kitchen.

I go back to the pan and keep stirring the oats into the sticky mixture.

'What are you making?' Violet looks over my shoulder.

'Flapjacks.' I wave a sticky hand at the recipe book. 'With Belgian chocolate on top.'

'Yum,' Violet says. She reaches behind the

bookstand and picks up a tin that I hadn't noticed was there. 'Look,' she says, reading the label. 'Caramel. I love caramel.' She hesitates. 'Maybe you could add some of that too.'

'Maybe,' I say. 'Can you grab me that tin?'

'Sure.' She hands me a rectangular cake tin that I've already lined with baking paper. I scoop in the clumpy mixture and pat it down with the wooden spoon. When it's all spread out and flat, I carry the tin over to the cooker.

'How long does it need to cook for?'

I glance over at the book. 'Twenty-five minutes.' She opens up the oven and sets the timer. I put the tin inside. 'Would you like some tea?' Violet asks. 'Or there's hot chocolate. I *can* boil a kettle.'

'Yeah, hot chocolate sounds good.' I wash my hands at the sink.

Violet fills the kettle and switches it on. I find the cupboard with the mugs. Mrs Simpson's mugs are pretty, all different colours of stoneware, some with stripes and polka dots. I give Violet a purple mug and use a blue one for me. She finishes making the hot chocolate and brings it over to the table. We sit facing each other.

'Look, I'm sorry about earlier,' I say. 'It's just . . . well . . .' The words stick to the roof of my mouth. 'Lots of things.'

'No worries,' she says. 'I'm the one who should

be sorry.'

Something unspoken seems to pass between us – one of those weird moments where you just know what the other person's thinking, and you don't have to bother with talking. But then it's gone, as Violet asks the question I've been expecting.

'So, your mum's really that blogger?'

'Yeah.' *That* blogger. Enough said.

'I hadn't heard of the blog, but Gretchen showed me. She said you guys used to be friends, but then when your mum got famous, you started acting all stuck-up.'

'Stuck-up?' I stare at her dumbfounded. 'Me?'

'I said you didn't seem like that to me. And I read some of the blog.'

'You did?' I lean forwards, feeling tense.

'I know your mum doesn't mention your name. But everyone at school seems to know about it. I couldn't believe she wrote all that personal stuff about you. You know – the stuff about you washing your white underwear with black socks, giving your whole family head lice, and wetting the bed till you were eight.' Her face is solemn. 'I know how I would feel . . .'

'How?'

'Embarrassed,' she says immediately. 'And also kind of sad.'

I smile weakly. And then I find myself telling

Violet just how embarrassing and 'kind of sad' it is for me for real. I tell her about Stacie, and about how Gretchen and Alison pretended to be my friends, but really they were 'leaking' stuff to Mum. I tell her about the violin, the tap-dancing, and the 'Mum's Survival Kit'. Then, I tell her about Dad leaving, and about Mum's online 'victory' over him. I tell her how Mum's most popular posts are the ones about *Top ten reasons I wish I'd never had kids*; and where does that leave me? And when I've finished telling her all that, a tear falls into the lukewarm hot chocolate in the mug in front of me.

She puts a hand on my arm. 'I didn't tell anyone that you made the scones, Scarlett. Honest.' She hesitates. 'I wanted to, though. Because you should get the credit.'

'I know I'm being totally lame. But it's just that I don't want anything – *anything* – to get back to Mum. I can't stand her writing about me. I—' A sob escapes. 'I just hate it. Every week when her blog post goes up, I just want to crawl into a hole and die.'

'Have you told her?'

'Told her?' As soon as the words are out, I realize that, despite trying to be friendly, Violet will never understand. 'Yeah, I did try. I told her it made everyone laugh at me. I told her that I have no friends any more, and that I don't want to do anything if she's going to write about it.'

'So what happened?'

'We had a "discussion" about it. She told me her side – that she's working really hard to be successful with the blog, and get advertisers and stuff. She said that she wanted to have a job where she could support me and my sister without working long hours away from home. She tried to tell me all this stuff about online demographics and unique visitors – most of it, I didn't really understand. I told her that I supported her goals and stuff, but that the things she said really hurt sometimes. So, I thought we'd come to an "understanding". I felt good for a few days. Until the next post came out. Guess what it was about?'

'Your talk?'

'Bingo.' I sigh. 'It was called *The ungrateful teenage muse* or something like that. You can guess what it said.'

'Yeah.'

'The only thing that kind of works is doing nothing – and I mean nothing at all. No clubs, no activities, no friends, nothing. She can't get as much mileage out of boring as she can out of failure.'

'Must be pretty lonely.'

'I guess so.' I shrug.

Her heart-shaped face brightens as she smiles.

'It's good then that you're doing something about it.'

'Doing? What am I doing?'

'You're cooking.' She sniffs the air as the smell of baking flapjacks gets stronger and stronger.

I lean forward with a stab of real fear. 'Violet, please. I'm not really going to *do* anything. I can't – I mean, I'm breaking into my neighbour's house and using all her stuff. If Mum found out and wrote about it, I'd probably be arrested or something.'

'Well, I won't tell – on one condition.' Her smile grows mischievous.

'What's that?'

'I want to cook with you. We can teach ourselves – just us. It will be a secret.'

'But—' I open my mouth to protest. There are a thousand things wrong with the idea. Instead, just for a second, I let myself be swept along by Violet's enthusiasm. 'A cooking club?' I glance around me at the amazing kitchen, mulling over the idea.

'Yeah. A *secret* cooking club.'

'Hmm.' I stand up as the oven beeps that it's done. 'Can I think about it?'

12

A DASH OF FRIENDSHIP

The flapjacks turn honey-brown in the oven. I take them out quickly so they don't get burnt. They smell rich, buttery and delicious. I put the tin on a wire rack to cool. For the next step, Violet opens the tin of caramel and scoops it into a bowl while I melt the chocolate over a pan of hot water.

'I never really thought about trying to cook or bake anything before,' Violet says. She peers at a pencilled-in note in the margin of the recipe and then mixes some salt into the caramel. 'I mean, my mum used to cook everything, and I guess I always thought that there'd be time to learn—'

She stops. I pause in my stirring and look sideways at her. She bites her lip for a second, and then her mouth upturns in its usual amused expression. But her eyes don't look amused. She stares down at the caramel, swirling the wooden spoon through it absently. I want to ask her what's up, but just then I notice the chocolate has completely melted, so I take it off the hob.

'Quick,' I say, 'let's get this on before it starts to harden. You go first.' We both take our bowls over to the table where I've put the flapjacks to cool. Violet spoons an even layer of caramel over the top. I keep stirring the chocolate, and when she's done the whole pan, I spoon a thick layer on top. When I've finished, Violet uses the handle of the spoon to score something in the cooling chocolate:

The Secret Cooking Club

She hands me the spoon. I underline the words with a squiggle. It all seems very solemn and official. But just then, my stomach breaks the mood by rumbling loudly. 'It looks good,' I say. 'I can't wait to taste it.'

After we've tidied up the mess and the chocolate has set a little, I cut it into squares and serve up two squares on Mrs Simpson's rose-patterned china. Violet and I clink our mugs together. Then we each take a bite.

'Gosh.' Violet grins. 'It's good.'

'It *is* good.' I can hear the pride in my own voice. It's crunchy and gooey and I can taste both the chocolate and the caramel. It all melts together in my mouth. I've had flapjacks loads of times – the kind wrapped in plastic from the corner shop. But this is completely different. This is home-made. And *I* made it. *We*. I take another bite, chewing it slowly. Part of me almost wants to tell Mum. *Almost*.

I lick a streak of chocolate off my lips. 'What are we going to do with them?' I say. 'We can't eat them all.'

'I could have a good go,' Violet jokes. Then her smile wavers. 'But I guess it's up to you.'

'No. It's up to *us*.' I savour the word. 'We're a club now.'

Violet takes a bite, chewing thoughtfully. 'I know you've got issues about it. But I really liked giving out the free samples at school. It was weird, but it made everybody a little bit nicer somehow.'

'Nicer?'

'Yeah. I think so. And if we did it again, we can say they were made by The Secret Cooking Club.' Violet wipes her chin. 'It'll seem like there are lots of us doing it.'

'You mean, like we're some kind of underground network who are all taking turns making things?'

Violet's eyes shine. 'It would be cool, wouldn't it? Especially if what we make actually tastes good. And just about anything is bound to taste better than canteen food.' She sticks out her tongue. 'That rice pudding they serve every other day tastes like sick.'

'It looks like it as well,' I giggle. 'All those lumps.'

'Gross!' She laughs too. 'So, you're in?'

'Well . . .' I have to admit, the idea does sound cool. And if a little sugar rush makes school a happier place, then who am I to complain?

'Unless you have a better idea?'

'I don't,' I say. 'Though I did think that maybe we could bake something for Mrs Simpson. If she's still in hospital, she must be hating the food too. We could take her a tin of flapjacks.'

'That's a great idea.' Violet says. 'Let's do it.'

'But I like your idea about school too,' I say. 'As long you solemnly swear on your life that no one will know I'm involved.'

'OK,' Violet says. 'I swear.' We shake sticky hands to seal the deal. Then we eat another square each and drink another mug of hot chocolate.

'Um, Violet,' I say, licking the crumbs from my lips. 'I think we might need another batch.'

A NAMELESS GIFT

Violet and I make two more batches of flap-jacks, chatting about all the things we could make next. The possibilities are endless, and it's nice to have someone who's as excited as I am. As I'm spreading the final layer of chocolate over the salted caramel, Violet comes over to the table with a little jar. 'I found these,' she says. 'Crystallized Violets. It says on the jar that they're real flowers.'

The jar is filled with sparkly purple flower petals coated with glittered sugar. I open the jar and hold it up to my nose. They smell very sweet.

'Do you want to put them on top?' I say.

'Well, I don't know. It might make for kind of funny flapjacks. But it could throw people off the scent that you had anything to do with it.'

'OK. Let's do it.'

Violet arranges the crystallized violets in a swirl pattern. The purple sparkles look like magic dust. I don't know how it's going to taste, but Violet seems to have a flair for making things look pretty.

We put the flapjacks for Mrs Simpson into Violet's Easter basket. For the school ones, we fill up a big tin with a picture of Peter Rabbit on it that we found in a cupboard. I wrap up the last two flapjacks in kitchen roll for Violet and me to take home. I leave the little notebook of recipes on the bookstand – it seems to have done a pretty good job keeping our secret so far, and it belongs in Rosemary's Kitchen.

We're in the middle of cleaning up when there's a muffled ringing sound. Violet's mobile phone. She checks the screen and gasps. 'It's seven o'clock already. I have to go.'

'Seven?' I can't believe it's that late. I was planning to tell Mum that I'd gone to the library again, but it closes at five. The words flash in my head: *Psst . . . my daughter went missing for two hours – was she: (a) smoking; (b) snogging; (c) drinking; (d) shoplifting?*

I'll have to think of something else.

I quickly finish the washing-up while Violet wipes down the worktop. Whatever spell we've been under is broken. Now, all the problems with our 'plan' seep into my head. What if the hospital won't let us in? What if Mrs Simpson is in a coma – or dead? What if someone at school sees me or Violet putting out the flapjacks? What if the crystallized violets taste disgusting? *What if? What if—?*

'I'm not sure about this,' I say. My chest feels like it's being squeezed by a giant fist.

'It will be OK,' Violet says. 'I promise. Let's just have a go.'

I force myself to take a breath. 'OK.'

THE BIG LAUGH-IN

When I get home, there's no sign that Mum's even noticed that I was gone. Kelsie's sitting in front of the TV watching *The Ice Princess*, her eyes glued to the screen. Her mouth is crusted with dried chocolate from a half-eaten pack of Hobnobs. The door to the Mum Cave is shut. I unwrap the flapjack, cut it into two pieces, and set it on a plate in the kitchen. I don't have my school bag or my homework, so I sit on the sofa next to my sister and eat a bag of prawn cocktail crisps.

As I'm trying to tune out my sister's off-key rendition of the theme song, all of a sudden Mum bursts into the room.

'Flapjacks!' she cries. 'I've been absolutely craving flapjacks all day. I mean, I didn't know it was flapjacks I wanted exactly . . .' She brushes a strand of unwashed hair off her face. 'But where on earth did they come from?'

'From me,' I say. 'Some kids at school made them. They were giving out free samples.'

'I love the purple sparkly things,' Mum says, chomping happily at her piece of flapjack. 'And the caramel. It reminds me of something else my grandma—' Frowning, she cuts herself off. 'You should do something like that, Scarlett.' She looks down at the empty bag of crisps in my lap. The cogs in her brain are clearly ticking. *Help! There's a new cooking club at school and my lazy, deadbeat daughter won't get off her bottom and stop eating crisps.*

'Yeah, Mum,' I say with a shrug. 'I probably should.'

At school the next day, I sit at the back of the maths lesson, watching Gretchen and Alison text each other under the table. Just before lunchtime, Violet raises her hand and asks to go to the toilet. She gives me a quick glance on her way out of the room. I feel a little thrill of fear and anticipation.

In the canteen, I sit at a corner table and watch the kids coming in – some with their lunch bags, others taking a tray and getting a hot dinner (some kind of chicken goopy stuff with clumpy bread pudding for dessert) from the window. While on her 'toilet break', Violet has placed the tin with the flapjacks on the centre table with a little sign that says 'Free Samples from *The Secret Cooking Club*'. Violet herself comes into the canteen a few minutes later, flanked by a laughing Gretchen and Alison. I deliberately look away from them.

Someone approaches the basket – none other than Nick Farr. My breath catches; he's so scrummy! His almond-shaped brown eyes widen. He looks around quickly and takes another piece. And then I find that he's looking in my direction and smiling.

OMG. Nick Farr is looking at me. He's walking towards me. Somehow he knows – he must. He . . .

. . . walks past me and sits down at a nearby table with a group of his friends. I exhale sharply. What was I thinking?

'Check this out,' he says to his mates, pointing at the centre table. 'The Secret Cooking Club.'

'Killer,' one of them replies. He and another mate stand up and walk to the centre table. They each grab a little piece of flapjack and eat it, and then another. Another of Nick's mates comes up and pretends he's going to grab the whole tin and stick it under his shirt. More people come up in a steady stream: two girls with pierced noses who are part of the goth crowd, three star rugby players, two girls on the swimming team, a couple of computer geeks, and then, horning their way to the front of the queue, Gretchen and Alison.

Gretchen wrinkles her pert little upturned nose as she looks inside the tin. Her voice is high-pitched enough that I can hear her over the din. 'What are those things on top?' she says to Alison.

'I don't know. But if I eat any of them, my face will break out in spots!'

The girls make a point of flouncing off without trying any flapjacks. Their rejection ruins the mood. Except for the computer geeks who come back for seconds, the crowd begins to dwindle.

Suddenly, from one of the far tables across the room, there's a loud snort of laughter. A few people turn to look. It's a tall girl with a neon-pink streak in her black hair. She's one of the goth crowd. They aren't the kind of kids who ever smile, but that's exactly what they're doing. The girl whispers to her friend, and feeds her a tiny piece of flapjack.

'OMG, it's fab,' the friend says. Before I know it, everyone's chattering and laughing, and people are splitting their flapjacks apart to make sure that everyone can try them. The good feeling seems to move like a chain reaction from one to the other.

From person to person, table to table. The sugar rush seems to be making everyone happy.

Gretchen looks at Alison. I can tell they're on the verge of trying to ruin everything by acting like everyone is totally lame, but then Nick comes up and whispers something in Gretchen's ear. Gretchen gives him a flirty smile and goes back to the centre table and takes a flapjack. I watch as the transformation comes over her – she goes back to Nick and whispers something in his ear, and they both start laughing their heads off. It's so loud that two teachers come in. They glance around, looking surprised, and then they smile too. The flapjack basket empties quickly, but the positive vibe is still there in the room. I'm even more shocked to realize that I'm smiling at the whole ridiculous thing. I spot Violet standing near the door. She's not laughing, but her bow-shaped lips are turned upwards in satisfaction. I walk towards her, but just then the bell rings, and by the time I get over to the door, she's gone.

MRS SIMPSON

The flapjacks are long gone, but that afternoon, there's still a lively buzz in the classroom – more people than usual speaking up and asking questions in class; talking to people they wouldn't normally, and generally more smiles all around. When it's time to go home, I meet up with Violet in the corridor. She's got the basket over her arm, and together we push through the crowds to the front entrance, and out to the car park.

'Everyone *loved* the flapjacks,' she says. 'Just like we hoped.'

'I know. I didn't expect people to like them quite so much.' I shiver a little knowing that *Nick* liked them.

Maybe it was the crystallized violets,' she says with a grin.

'Well, they definitely made a change from that gross bread pudding!'

'That's for sure,' Violet says. 'Anyway, we'd better get going.'

'Going? Where are we going?'

'To see Mrs Simpson, remember? Do you know which hospital she's in?' Violet's question throws me.

'Um, no.'

'Well, the Royal Elmsbury is closest, so let's try there first. There's a bus, I think.'

'OK.' I shrug, knowing that Violet's right. Flap-jacks or no, visiting Mrs Simpson is the right thing to do. 'Let's go.'

The bus stop is around the corner from the school, and we don't have to wait long. Twenty minutes later, the bus drops us off in front of the hospital. It's a busy, intimidating place, with cars and vans coming and going, old people and pregnant women meandering across the zebra crossing; people in wheelchairs; and nurses in uniforms going in and out.

Violet leads the way inside. There's a gift shop and a coffee kiosk in the lobby and at one side, a reception desk. Violet goes up to the receptionist and speaks confidently, like she's been in a hospital loads of times and isn't even a little bit scared.

'We're here to visit a patient,' she says. 'Mrs Simpson.'

The woman looks over her half-moon glasses at Violet and me. 'Which ward is she in?'

'I'm not sure.' Violet looks at me.

'Her name is Rosemary Simpson,' I say, trying to sound like a grown-up. 'Can you direct us to the right ward?'

The woman types something into the computer one finger at a time. It seems to take an age. Finally, she looks up again. 'Are you relations?'

'Yes,' I say without hesitation. 'I'm her niece. She's my only aunt, and I'm really worried about her. My friend and I brought her a basket of sweets we made.'

The woman frowns. 'She's in the Hessel Wing. Follow the blue line to B ward.'

We follow the painted blue line on the floor through bleak corridors; past outpatients hurrying to appointments in worrying-sounding departments such as oncology, radiotherapy, physical rehabilitation and ante-natal. With our basket and school bags, Violet and I are like two Little Red Riding Hoods wandering through a scary forest of machines, fluorescent lights and sick people. Finally, the blue line ends in a door marked Hessel

Wing, Ward B. I push open the heavy swinging door.

Inside is another reception desk with two nurses in pale blue uniforms. One is riffling through paperwork, the other is typing on a computer. I'm relieved when Violet goes up to the desk. She says who we are, and who we're here to see.

'Rosemary Simpson?' The nurse with the paperwork looks at the other nurse. 'Is she allowed visitors?'

'I suppose so,' the other woman says, still staring at the computer screen. 'But she's been given a mild sedative. She has concussion and needs to be kept here under observation.'

'Can we see her?' I say. 'We brought her a basket with some flapjacks that we made.'

'She won't be eating any flapjacks. But since you're relations' – the nurse eyes me sceptically – 'you can have five minutes to see her. And you can leave the basket here if you like.'

I sense that if we leave the flapjacks, she and the other nurse will hoover up what's inside. Violet obviously thinks the same as she clutches the basket even more tightly.

The nurse points down the corridor. 'She's in room six. Be back here in five minutes.'

'Five minutes,' I repeat. Violet and I walk

quickly down the hall. 'What a horrible place,' I whisper.

Violet doesn't answer. She seems lost in a world of her own. 'Yeah,' she says finally as we reach the door to room six. A gameshow theme is blaring loudly from inside.

I peer inside the room. There are two raised beds, one on each side of the room. In the bed nearest the door is a white-haired woman who's staring at the television and eating a heart-shaped box of bonbons. There are lots of flowers and get-well cards on the bedside table. Clearly, she's being well looked after. In the other bed is a grey figure, little more than a lump underneath the thin, blue blanket. There's a breathing tube sticking out of her nose, an IV in her arm, and she's hooked up to a monitor that is blipping slowly in the corner. There are no flowers or get-well cards anywhere.

I walk into the room. 'Shh,' the white-haired woman says. 'They're about to solve the puzzle.'

On the television screen, a woman is turning over the letters in a puzzle. 'Bad luck,' the host says to the losing contestant.

'Pah, it wasn't bad luck at all – he was just thick,' the old woman says, gesturing with the heart-shaped box. Her accent sounds Scottish or Northern or something. She glowers, as if noticing

Violet and me for the first time. 'Who are you?'

'We're looking for Mrs Simpson. Is that her?' I point to the blanket bulge, already knowing the answer.

'What's left of her.' The old woman frowns.

'We brought this.' Violet holds up the basket on her arm. 'We thought she might be sick of hospital food.'

The woman pops a bonbon in her mouth. 'Nice of you, pet, I'm sure. But I don't think she'll be up to it any time soon.'

'Has she been awake?' I ask.

The woman flips through the TV channels with the remote. 'Oh aye,' she says, her eyes wide. 'She's been awake – off and on. And let me tell you, it's hard to get any sleep when she is.' She shakes her head and tsks. 'Tussling with the blankets and moaning about her cat. She wants to go home, but her nephew won't have it.'

'Nephew?' Violet asks.

'You mean Mr Kruffs?' I say.

'Aye, that's him. So you know him, do you?'

'No, but I've seen the election posters—'

'Election.' She snorts. 'Well, good luck to him, that's all I can say. Swanning in here, making her upset. I've thought about asking to be moved rooms, but in here' – she laughs grimly – 'one old dear is as good as the next.' She settles on a channel and turns up the volume. 'At least she's asleep most of the time.'

From the other bed there's a loud groan and a rustling noise. The grey old woman under the blanket coughs and splutters, then wriggles in the bed like she's trying to prop herself up on her elbows. Her eyes are open, but glassy, like she's not really seeing anything in the room. Her head turns slightly and she spies the basket. She leans forward and sniffs the air. Her blue eyes meet mine.

'Mrs Simpson?' I whisper. 'We've made you some flapjacks. They're chocolate and salted caramel.'

The old woman sinks back into the bed. Her eyes close again, her lips drawn into a thin line. But then she seems to smile. Her breathing grows even as she goes back to sleep.

'Maybe she'll be able to try them later,' I say to Violet in a low voice. Violet nods and sets the basket down on Mrs Simpson's bedside table. I reach out and touch Mrs Simpson's gnarled hand. 'Get well soon,' I whisper.

Violet and I tiptoe out of the room.

16

BANOFFEE

Violet and I don't say much as we ride the bus back. I secretly vow to avoid hospitals in the future at all costs. I keep thinking about Mrs Simpson – a helpless bulge under a thin blanket. I know it was the right thing to visit her, but I kind of wish we hadn't. I'd rather think of Rosemary Simpson as the amazing cook with the fabulous kitchen. She did seem to revive a little when she smelt the flapjacks, though. I hope she gets to taste them.

Violet stares out of the window of the bus. As the sky grows darker and her reflection in the window sharpens, I'm startled to see a tear trickling down her cheek. I turn away so as not to embarrass her. The bus stops near the school and we both get off.

'So I guess I'll see you tomorrow?' I try hard to sound cheery.

She shrugs. The tears are gone but there are dark hollows under her eyes. 'OK.'

I wait for her to turn round or walk off – I don't even know where she lives – but she keeps on walking along beside me.

I turn down my road. We walk together, passing several houses with 'Emory Kruffs for MP' signs in their windows. We reach the last two houses at the end of the terrace: my house, and Mrs Simpson's.

'I'm going inside to feed the cat,' I announce.

Violet looks at me. She smiles.

I unlock Mrs Simpson's door and we go inside. Right away, I can tell that something's wrong.

'Where's the cat?' I whisper. My skin prickles with goosebumps.

'Maybe it's asleep?'

'But it's always been here before.'

Inside, there's no sign of the cat, and other things are different too. Mrs Simpson's pictures have been taken off the wall and stacked against each other, and a lot of her knick-knacks have been cleared away. There are a few open boxes with bubble wrap spilling out. Mrs Simpson is obviously in no state for spring cleaning, so it can only be one person – Mr Kruffs. The idea that he's been here gives me the shivers.

Violet seems to have the same thought. 'What if he's still here?' she says guardedly.

We stand still, listening for sounds from upstairs or inside the kitchen. Everything is quiet.

I square my shoulders. 'We're not doing anything wrong. We're only here to feed the cat.'

'Maybe we should leave.'

'I'm staying,' I say. 'We may never get another chance to be here. You can go if you want to.' I give her a sideways glance. 'But I'd rather you didn't.'

Her violet eyes widen with shared understanding. 'OK,' she says. 'What shall we make tonight?'

The kitchen has avoided being ransacked, but only just. The cat's bed and food dish are gone – at least whoever took it away is going to feed it. There are other things different too: dirty teacups in the sink, a list of 'house clearance' firms on the worktop, and the little book of recipes is off its wooden bookstand. I notice how tattered its binding is; how faded the cover. It's covered with crumbs, like someone used it for a cutting board to make a sandwich on.

I pick up the book and blow off the crumbs. I set it back on the bookstand and open it up at random. It falls open almost automatically to a recipe for 'Georgie Porgie's Banoffee Pie'.

'Banoffee Pie!' Violet says. 'That's my favourite pudding in the whole world.'

I lower my eyes. 'I don't think I've ever had it.' I skim over the ingredients. Banana and toffee – not two things I would ever have thought of putting together – plus lots of cream.

'Are you serious?! Then we have to make it!'

Violet's excitement wins me over – that, and the fact that there's a fruit bowl in the centre of the table that has a big bunch of fresh bananas in it. Some things are just meant to be, I guess.

'OK.' I say, 'Let's do it.'

The rest of the ingredients aren't so neatly lined up this time. It's like the magic kitchen elves have all fled from Mr Kruffs. We have to dig through the cupboards to find a packet of oaty biscuits, a can of condensed milk, and a half-used packet of brown sugar. In the very back of the fridge, we find the double cream and butter.

When everything is assembled I read through the recipe again. 'Look at him,' Violet says over my shoulder, pointing to the cartoon-like picture of fat little Georgie Porgie. He's chasing a flock of merry girls with his lips pursed in a kiss. 'He's gross.' She makes a face. 'I wouldn't want him to kiss me. Unless he happened to grow up to be a boy like Nick Farr.'

My insides judder. 'Nick Farr?'

'He's cute, isn't he?' She laughs.

'Yeah.' There seems no point in lying.

I turn on the hob ready to melt the butter. For some reason, I feel kind of nervous and on edge – it could be the hospital visit, or the intruder that was here. But if I'm honest, it's probably Violet's mention of Nick Farr.

Violet squishes the biscuits into crumbs and tips them into the pan. As I stir them into the butter, I begin to feel a little calmer.

'Do you think he'll come back?' Violet says.

'Who?' I say, startled.

'Mr Kruffs. It's kind of creepy that he's been here.'

I look around Rosemary's Kitchen. It seems lonely without the cat. 'Maybe Mr Kruffs has permission to be here, I don't know . . .' I trail off. 'I wish there was something we could do to help Mrs Simpson.'

Violet brings over some tart tins from the cupboard. We press the crumbly mixture in the bottom, and then put the whole thing in the fridge to set. 'Like what?' she says.

I shake my head. 'Right now, I don't have a clue.'

SECRET SAMPLES

I really don't know what to do about Mrs Simpson. But I do know that making the banoffee pie is a blast. Violet and I triple the recipe – so we have enough for us plus lots of 'free samples' for school. Luckily, Rosemary's Kitchen has plenty of bowls and tart tins.

Making the filling is sweet and sticky and messy and fun. We gorge ourselves on bananas and licking out the bowls. Then we chat and laugh and look through the cupboards while the pies set in the fridge. I find several large chocolate bars and take them out.

'The recipe says to decorate the pies with

chocolate curls,' I say, pointing to the book.

'We can use these too,' Violet takes out a tin of baking decorations – sprinkles of all sizes and colours, icing bags and colours, even gold leaf you can eat.

When the pies have chilled we take them out one by one – two round ones, and two that we made in tins shaped like a heart and a gingerbread man. 'Look, it's Georgie Porgie,' I say when I take the swirly banana cream man out of the fridge. We both laugh.

I make the chocolate curls using a vegetable peeler like the recipe book says to do. Violet decorates Georgie Porgie with little icing stars, and a tie made of multicoloured sprinkles. She gives him eyes of chocolate buttons, and an icing nose and mouth. I can't help laughing as I add his hair of chocolate curls – I've never seen such a fancy pie before, and Georgie Porgie looks nothing like Nick Farr. Violet laughs too, and gives him a collar and belt of crystallized violets. He ends up looking like a big, goopy snowman.

On the heart-shaped pudding, Violet writes 'The Secret Cooking Club' in big, loopy icing letters and I cover the rest in sprinkles and chocolate curls. Finally, we're done.

'They look fab,' I say, beaming. We find some deep Tupperware cake containers to use to take the pies to school tomorrow. Then we tuck in and eat the little round one we've made for ourselves.

The pie is gooey and moist, and the taste of toffee and fresh banana seems like the most natural combination of flavours in the whole world.

'Mm,' Violet purrs, taking a bite. 'This is the best.'

I let cool sweet cream settle on my tongue for a second before swallowing. It's lovely and sweet, but not too sweet – like Goldilocks's porridge, it's just right. I still can't believe we've made it ourselves. But we did!

'We'll need plastic bowls and spoons for school.' I lick the cream off my upper lip. 'It's pretty gooey.'

'Yeah,' Violet says between bites. 'We can get them at the newsagents on the way to school. Do you have any money?'

'I've got a bit saved up from my pocket money. I could use that.'

We clean everything up and put the pies back in Mrs Simpson's fridge to chill overnight. We agree that I'll come and get them tomorrow before school.

It's dark by the time we leave the house, and stepping outside is like plunging into a cold bath. Nothing seems real to me any more other than Rosemary's Kitchen. Violet seems unusually quiet, like she feels the same as me.

'You OK?' I ask. We stand at the dim edge of a circle of street light.

'Yeah.' Violet nods. 'See you tomorrow.' She turns and starts walking. I stand there watching her go until she turns the corner and disappears.

This time when I get home, I'm not so lucky as before. Mum is in the kitchen, frantically ringing people on her mobile, looking for me.

'Seriously, Scarlett,' she says, 'I was worried sick. Where have you been?'

I sit down at the table, feeling exhausted. I wish I could tell Mum everything – about the hospital, the cooking, Mrs Simpson and how we have to save her from Mr Kruffs. And about the scrummy banoffee pie we made. I open my mouth and close it again. I can't tell Mum anything. If I do, I'll only regret it.

'Sorry, Mum,' I say, half meaning it. 'There's a new girl at school – I went over to her house. We're working on a project together for science.'

Mum doesn't ask the girl's name, and I don't volunteer it. She shakes her head. 'Honestly, Scarlett – I mean, I know you don't want to talk to me any more, but you really can't do that kind of thing.'

'I'm sorry, Mum. It's just that . . .' I take a breath. I'm going to tell her how I feel. I'm going to see if we can be friends again. I'm going to—

'Don't do it again.' Her face is red as she checks her watch. 'I'm so behind – my guest post for *scarykids.com* is due tomorrow. I just can't believe how thoughtless you are sometimes.'

She turns and blusters off into the Mum Cave. The door slams behind her. With a big sigh, I go upstairs to my room and crawl into bed. I dream of a flock of girls chasing a cream-pie-shaped Nick Farr, whose eyes meet mine as he runs away.

The next morning I wake up with butterflies in my stomach. I find my pocket money tin in my sock drawer and open it up. There are a few loose coins in the bottom but the five-pound note I had inside is gone. I groan softly. Not only does Mum often forget to give me my pocket money, but she's always 'borrowing' money from me when she forgets to go to the cashpoint.

Snores are coming from Mum's room, and I don't want to wake her. Instead, I head downstairs to the Mum Cave where Mum keeps her purse. As usual, her desk is a mess. There are papers everywhere – crumpled drafts of articles and blog posts, letters from Boots and glossy photos of the Survival Kit packaging. I'm struck by how hard Mum is working to keep her blog empire going.

I find Mum's handbag and 're-borrow' a five-pound note, scribbling on a yellow sticky to let her know. Underneath the bag there's a piece of paper – a printout of something she's writing, half of which is crossed out in red pen. My stomach knots as I skim over the uncrossed-out bit.

Me against her – why have we grown so apart?

It starts out in a joking tone – stuff like: 'I never wanted to be one of those pushy parents. But now I see I messed up big time. I mean, if I'd known that my daughter was going to hate me by the time she was a teenager, I should have made sure that she was a concert pianist.'

I read on. Instead of going into the usual stuff, I'm surprised by what she's written. 'Lately, something weird has happened. I've started remembering what it was like to be *her* age. It started when, all of a sudden, I had a craving for macaroni cheese – the way my grandma used to make it. And I got to wondering: how does *she* feel, and have I really been paying attention . . . ?'

The paragraph is scribbled out in red pen. But the words are there in black and white.

IN THE HALL . . .

Violet is waiting for me in front of the newsagents. I've got the three Tupperware containers in a huge hessian bag I found in Rosemary's Kitchen. We've got just enough money to buy a pack of plastic bowls and spoons, and some baking powder which we're almost out of at Mrs Simpson's.

'It's your turn today,' she says as we're on our way out.

'My turn? For what?'

'To set up the secret samples. You just have to make sure you get to the canteen before everyone else. And don't forget to make a sign to put on the table.'

'Me?' My heart thuds in alarm. 'I thought you were going to do it.'

'I did it last time – I mean, I can't go to the toilet every day at the same time, can I?'

'I don't know.' We walk on in silence as worry fizzes in my veins. What if someone notices me sneaking three creamy mountains of banoffee pie into the canteen? Word travels fast around school. It isn't just me that I'm worried about, but The Secret Cooking Club. It may just be Violet and me, but if I lose that, then what's left?

The morning flies by. I try to focus on learning adverbs and then algebra, but I keep staring at the clock as it gets nearer and nearer to the time when I'm supposed to raise my hand and ask if I can go to the toilet. Twenty minutes to go, then ten, then five.

Just as I'm about to raise my hand, Nick Farr beats me to it.

'Sorry, Mrs Fry, but I need the loo,' he says.

The maths teacher gets a boys' loo pass down from the wall and hands it to him.

'Uh, me too,' I say in a small voice. I can feel the redness creeping over my face as someone behind me sniggers.

The teacher puts her hands on her hips. 'Lunch is in fifteen minutes – can't you wait?'

'No, Mrs Fry.' My skin crawls with the eyes of everyone looking at me. When the banoffee pie turns up in the kitchen, surely everyone will know it's me.

But what can I do? I look pleadingly in Violet's direction, but she's staring down at her notebook, her blue-black hair a curtain in front of her face. With an irritated sigh, the teacher gives me a girls' loo pass. I hold my breath until I'm across the room and out the door.

The corridor is empty – no sign of Nick. I hurry down the hall to the empty classroom where I've stowed the hessian bag of banoffee pies in the coat cupboard. They're right where I left them, along with the bag of plastic bowls and spoons. I scoop everything up and go back into the corridor. I rush past the loos towards the canteen. If anyone spots me now—

A door swooshes open just behind me.

— I'm sunk!

I can feel eyes on my back. *His* eyes. Nick Farr. Captain of the rugby team, star science student, good friend of Gretchen, Alison and all the popular girls. Fancied by the rest of us from afar – but in this case, not far enough.

'Scarlett?'

His voice.

'You OK?'

I turn round, my eyes wide like a deer in the headlamps.

'Yeah, fine.' I force a smile.

He stares at the big bag in my hand.

'What have you got there?'

'Um, nothing.' Before he can say another word, I go into the girls' loos. I stand there, panting, looking at my reflection in the mirror. My hair is looking as frazzled as I feel, and the skin of my neck is covered with guilty-looking red blotches. My mind is a whirlwind of indecision. Do I go back to the empty classroom and hide the goods? Do I continue with my mission like nothing's happened? Do I tell Violet? Try to talk to Nick and see if he'll keep the secret? Or maybe he won't put two and two together. OK, that's pretty unlikely.

I smooth my hair and scowl at my reflection. 'Get a grip,' I say to the girl staring back.

The hallway is empty when I leave the loos. I rush to the canteen; my hand is shaking as I take out the pies and set them out in a row on the table. The dinner ladies are talking loudly behind their little window as they do the final preparations for lunch, but they don't notice me. I get the bowls and spoons out of the bag – why didn't I take them out of the packaging before I got here? – and manage to wrestle them out of the plastic wrapping, ripping a fingernail in the process. Finally, I unfold my sign and tape it to the edge of the table: 'Free samples – from *The Secret Cooking Club*.'

I turn and run out of the canteen and back down the corridor. I slip back into the classroom as everyone is putting away their notebooks before lunch. As I reach my seat, I can't help looking to the front of the room – where Nick Farr sits. He turns round in his seat and his eyes meet mine, just like in my dream. My stomach turns over. He gives me a wide, melting grin . . . then puts a finger to his lips.

19

THE SECRET COOKING CLUB STRIKES AGAIN

There's a rush of fluttering papers and scraping chairs as the class breaks for lunch. Violet gives me a knowing look from across the room, and then goes to join Gretchen and Alison. I feel a stab of jealousy, but part of our 'cover' is that Violet and I won't hang out together at school. I follow the crowds of kids to the canteen.

I sit down at my usual table near the door. A number of people are already queuing at the centre table, waiting to take a bowl of banoffee pie. It's the same as before – the goths, the sports crowd, the geeks. My heart lurches as Gretchen pushes her way to the front of the queue, flanked by Alison and Violet.

But if anyone was expecting another laugh-in, they're in for a surprise. One of the goth girls – tall and skinny with dark black eyeliner – elbows Gretchen out of the way. 'There's a queue, you know,' she says tersely.

I hold my breath as Gretchen turns to face the girl, craning her neck upwards. 'What did you say?' she challenges.

The tall girl snorts. Two of her pale-faced friends come up on either side of her like twin wraiths. 'Wait your turn.'

'Get over yourself,' Gretchen says. Her face has a strange greyish tinge to it – is she sick?

The tall girl glances at her two friends, glares at Gretchen, and gives a little snort. 'You know what?' she says, flicking her hand. 'You go ahead – be my guest.'

Gretchen gives her a fake little PTA princess smile. She takes a big goopy piece of pie. Everyone is watching as she holds the plastic spoon to her nose, sniffs it, then takes a bite.

'Hah,' the tall girl says. 'You're going to get so *fat*.'

The last word seems to echo around the room. For what seems like eternity, no one speaks, or even breathes.

If there's a word in the English language for the

colour of Gretchen's face, then I'm sure I don't know it. At first, it turns kind of pink and spotty like she's been scratching a patch of eczema or something, but then it immediately turns a shade of greenish grey like pea soup left in the fridge too long. The spoon in her hand drops to the floor. Everybody turns to stare as her cheeks get all full and puffy and her eyes bulge out from her face. 'Watch out,' Violet cries. But before anyone can even react, Gretchen's mouth opens and a volcano of vomit erupts, flying across the table and landing in a slick, brown mess all over the floor.

There's a collective gasp of horror. And then the tall goth girl shrieks, 'Oh, gross – it's Retchin' Gretchen!'

'Retchin' Gretchen.' The words move through the canteen like a Chinese whisper. There's the odd groan and trickles of laughter, and a growing sense of mayhem. Out of the corner of my eye, I see Violet sneak out of the room. I get up and run after her.

Outside the canteen, I slump against the wall. 'What have we done?' I hiss at the same time she blurts out, 'Our lovely pie!'

'That was so awful,' I say, not sure whether I feel like laughing or crying. 'We never should have given out free samples. I mean – do you think Gretchen's OK?'

Violet shrugs. 'I think so. And it wasn't our pie that made her sick – she had a stomach ache earlier.' Her eyes grow wide. 'Retchin' Gretchen.' Laughter sputters from her mouth.

The canteen begins to empty in a mass exodus. I notice that, despite Gretchen's retchin', quite a few people are carrying bowls of banoffee pie.

'I'll see you after school, OK?' Violet says.

'I don't know . . .' I begin walking off down the corridor so that no one will see us talking. Now that our pie has humiliated Gretchen, she'll want to know who's involved. How could I ever have allowed myself to get into this situation?

'Come on, Scarlett!' Violet says.

'Look,' I say, 'I can't do this any more. If my mum finds out—'

'So that's it then?' Violet interrupts. 'You're just going to let her win? Like you've been doing all along?'

I whirl around to face her, my anger boiling. 'You just don't get it, do you? And luckily for you – you never will.'

THE BETRAYAL

The only thing worse than not having anything good in my life, is having something and then losing it. Thanks to Gretchen and my rift with Violet, The Secret Cooking Club dies a quick but painful death.

After school, instead of going to Mrs Simpson's house, I go to the library. I've always been good at school stuff, so I'm able to finish my homework quickly. I read through a couple of science magazines, trying to get interested in something. But all I can think about is how much I miss Violet, and which recipes we might have tried had things been different. I even forget to worry too much about

Mum's upcoming blog post. Even if she's somehow heard about Gretchen, there's nothing to link what happened to me.

Gretchen isn't at school the next day. Violet hangs out with Alison. The school is still buzzing about 'the incident', and phones get passed around with videos posted on YouTube. I even feel kind of sorry for Gretchen. *Kind of.*

On Friday morning, Mum's weekly blog post goes live. The title this week is *The Single Mum's Guide to Dating*. It's horrific and cringeworthy, but at least it isn't about me. Gretchen is back at school, her hair newly cut and her nails done in a perfect French manicure, acting for all the world like nothing happened.

At lunchtime, I watch from a distance as Violet talks and laughs with Gretchen, Alison and Nick like they've been friends for ever. Violet has chosen them. Now, the most I can hope for is that she forgets that I, and The Secret Cooking Club, ever existed.

After school I go to the library again – this time I've got an essay to write that I actually need to do some research for. I go there directly after school and stay until it closes. I wander home slowly, dreading the evening ahead, the weekend and, pretty much, the rest of my life.

It's almost dark by the time I turn on to my road.

I stop outside Mrs Simpson's house. The windows are covered, but I can just make out a sliver of light coming from inside. I creep up to the door and peek through the letter box. The light is coming from the partly ajar kitchen door. And then I hear laughter – girls' laughter.

My heart goes to my throat. Violet is inside. And she's with someone else – not one person, but two. 'Yummy!' a high voice squeals. I know that voice.

Gretchen.

I stand there frozen, unable to breathe. I'm not sure how much time goes by, but pretty soon I see the silhouettes of Gretchen and Alison against the cosy rectangle of light. I hear a chorus of 'bye's, 'thanks' and 'catch you later's. I rush away from the door and hide behind a smelly wheelie bin in the alleyway at the side of the house. The door opens and closes. Footsteps.

'That was actually fun.' A voice – Alison's.

'Yeah – I told you Violet was cool.'

My heart is thrumming so loud that I barely hear them walking off down the road. Whatever they were doing, Violet's stayed behind to clean up the mess. I storm up to the door and ring the bell – I hope it scares the pants off her.

There's no answer, so I kick away the mat, pick up the key and turn it roughly in the lock. I slam the door behind me as I go inside.

There's a sound in the kitchen of running footsteps. Violet must be trying to hide. I stomp in – let her think it's Mr Kruffs.

'Violet?' Instead of sounding menacing, my voice breaks.

There's no answer.

'How could you *do* it? We had a secret – together. How could you tell Gretchen – of all people?!' My voice catches again, and an instant later, I'm sobbing. 'I *trusted* you!'

Violet comes out from around the side of the bookcase. Her face seems thinner, and her eyes have dark circles underneath, like she hasn't slept.

'You said you didn't want to do this any more,' she says quietly. 'I came here yesterday after school *and* the day before and waited for you. But you didn't come.'

'So instead you brought Gretchen! You know how I feel about her. You brought her *here*!' The words gurgle from my mouth like poison. 'You betrayed me, Violet. You betrayed us.'

'No, I didn't.' She tries to put her hand on my arm but I jerk away. It's then that I notice the tray of undecorated cupcakes in frilly pink wrappings set out on a wire rack to cool. I clench my fists to keep from throwing them in the bin.

'Gretchen figured out it was me,' Violet blurts. 'That I was involved in The Secret Cooking Club. I mean, it was kind of obvious, wasn't it? The free samples started just about the time I joined the school.'

'So? You could have denied it.'

'No, I couldn't! Nick saw you in the corridor acting weird. Gretchen put two and two together, and figured out that you put the pies in the canteen.'

'No!' I put my hands over my face. 'That's exactly what I was afraid of.'

'Listen – OK? She thought The Secret Cooking Club was a really cool idea. She tried the flapjacks and loved them. And actually, she didn't get sick from the banoffee pie – she had a stomach bug.'

'That's rubbish.'

'I didn't know what to do. The secret was out. I knew you wouldn't want her to tell your mum.'

'My mum?' My whole body goes rigid.

'Yeah,' Violet says. 'So to make her keep the secret, I invited her and Alison to join.' Her shoulders slump. 'I saw where the key was kept so I knew I could get in . . . I know now it was a huge mistake but I didn't know what else to do. I knew you probably hated me for making you put the pies in the canteen. But even if you never came back, I wanted to keep the secret. I told Gretchen that she could never tell anyone that you were involved. That you hated what she did to you before. I . . .'

Her voice quavers. 'I thought I was doing you a favour . . .'

'A favour!' I cry. 'Is that what you call it? I poured out my heart to you – told you all about my stupid mum and how she makes me feel. And what do you do? Tell *Gretchen*, of all people!'

'I'm sorry, Scarlett.'

'I mean, how would you like it if your mum splashed your whole life over the web? How would you like it if your mum were like mine—?'

I stop abruptly. Violet turns away, her shoulders shaking as she begins to cry. All of a sudden, the penny drops. I've made a terrible mistake.

21

BUTTERCREAM

My anger dissolves in my throat. It all makes a kind of sad, tragic sense. For all my whingeing about my mum, Violet has never mentioned hers. And I've never asked. Aunt Hilda – why is Violet *living* with Aunt Hilda?

'My mum's dead,' Violet says. 'So's my dad. So you're right – I don't know exactly how you feel.'

'Oh, Violet.' I take a step backwards, astounded by the force of her revelation and, unwittingly, my own selfishness. She lifts her head and I put my arm over her shoulders. 'I'm so sorry,' I say.

Nodding, she wipes her eyes. I sit her down in one of the chairs. The cupcakes are cooling on a wire rack in front of us. I lean forward and examine them. Even un-iced, they look fluffy and delicious.

'Do you want to talk about it?' I say quietly.

She doesn't answer. Next to the cupcakes is a big bowl with a wooden spoon sticking out of it. She pulls the bowl in front of her and starts stirring – it's the icing for the cupcakes. A piping bag and a box of cake-decorating nozzles are set out on the table.

'We made these cupcakes for my birthday,' Violet explains. 'It's tomorrow.' Her lip quivers. 'I felt bad coming here without you, but I really thought you'd quit. I didn't want to lose this.' She gestures with the spoon. 'The Secret Cooking Club was important to me too.'

'I've been totally selfish,' I say. 'And I hope you can forgive me.'

She smiles faintly. 'Of course.'

'Can I help with the cupcakes?'

'Yeah.'

We split the icing into two separate bowls. I colour my half pink, and she adds clear white glitter to hers. I hand her the icing kit. The picture on the box shows that you can make little whirls and swirls with the icing bag. It looks kind of complicated, but I'm sure Violet can do it. She spoons some glitter icing into the bag and tries out some of the nozzles on a piece of kitchen roll. I smooth on a base layer of pink to each cupcake.

She takes one of the cupcakes I iced and begins making a little border of icing swirls around the edge. Then she puts a crystallized violet in the middle and surrounds it with crystallized rose petals. Finally, she tops it all off by sprinkling on pink edible glitter.

'It's so pretty,' I say.

'I love doing the piping.'

I hand her another cupcake. She changes nozzles and this time she makes a border like a ribbon. We work in silence for a few minutes.

'My parents were in a car accident,' she says finally. 'They were driving home from a church fundraiser and a drunk driver hit them head-on. Dad was killed straightaway. But Mum . . .' She sniffs. A tear trickles down her cheek. She stops piping the cupcakes and wipes her sleeve across her face. 'They thought she would be OK. She was in a coma. I moved in with Aunt Hilda and visited Mum every day in hospital and sat with her for hours. I talked to her, sang songs – stuff like that. I just wanted to do something to make her wake up.' She swallows hard. 'And then she did wake up. She didn't know who I was. They said she had "trauma to her brain and internal organs" but that in time she might recover. But as I was sitting there, the machine started beeping. She went into cardiac arrest. They did what they could, but nothing worked.'

'I'm so sorry.' As I say it again, I realize that 'sorry' must be the most useless word in the whole world. 'It must have been— I mean, so awful.'

She picks up the icing bag again. 'It was,' she says. 'I try not to think about it. But sometimes, I dream about that sound – when she flatlined.' Another tear dribbles down her face. She wipes it away quickly. 'I don't usually cry.'

'It's OK – really.' I give her another quick hug. 'And I'm so sorry that I've been whingeing about my mum, when at least she's—' I stop, worried that I've put my foot in it again.

'. . . alive,' Violet finishes for me. 'Don't worry about it.' She starts on the next cupcake. 'Your mum sounds pretty awful. I guess I'm lucky – Aunt Hilda's been really nice to me.' Her hand trembles and she blurs the border she's making. I smooth it over with a knife so she can start again. 'But she'll never be Mum.'

'Yeah,' I say stupidly. I remember the pang – the very brief pang – I felt when I saw the ambulance in our road and worried that maybe something had happened to Mum. When Dad left, I felt sad, and for a while I wondered if there was something

I could have done to be a better daughter so he would stay. But Dad had nearly always been at work or out with his mates; he'd never had much time for Kelsie and me, so it wasn't such a big change when he suddenly wasn't there. Kelsie was only a toddler so she barely even remembers him. But if something happened to Mum . . .

I shiver inwardly. She may not be perfect – far from it – but she's still my mum.

'Aunt Hilda had to take me because there was no one else. I don't think she really wanted to – I mean, she has her own life. She likes to go out with her friends after work, but she doesn't want to leave me alone. Plus, she got divorced a year or so ago, and she belongs to an internet dating site. I'm . . . you know . . . kind of in the way.'

'I'm sure that's not true.'

She shrugs. 'Whatever. At least I've got this.' She points to the cupcakes that look so beautifully white, pink and sparkly.

'Yeah.'

She looks up at me, her eyes the colour of a day-old bruise. 'So now you know. My life in a nutshell.'

I nod.

'So what do we do now?' she says. 'About The Secret Cooking Club? I need to know – are you still in?'

'Yeah,' I say, immediately. 'I'm still in.'

*

I'm still in.

Of course I am. Violet needs a friend as much as I do, and besides, The Secret Cooking Club is half me. Or . . . a quarter, now.

I lie awake in bed that night, unable to sleep. I still feel worried that Violet let Gretchen in on our secret – even if she meant well. When we'd finished the cupcakes and were cleaning up the kitchen, Violet assured me that Gretchen was totally on board and would keep things a secret. Alison wasn't a problem – she would do whatever Gretchen told her. She said she'd talk to Gretchen and Alison tomorrow, and we could all meet up on Sunday.

'OK,' I said, still sceptical. 'But if Gretchen tells anyone, then that's it – I'm out,' I warned. 'Do you understand?'

Violet said she understood.

She said she would take care of everything.

I have to believe her.

22

THE NEW SECRET COOKING CLUB

'Welcome to The Secret Cooking Club.' My voice comes out less steady than when I practised it. I force a smile as Violet comes into Mrs Simpson's kitchen followed by Gretchen and Alison.

Gretchen eyes me warily. 'Hello, Scarlett.'

'This is such a killer kitchen,' Alison says. 'It must be nice to have a super-blogger for a mum.'

I glance over at Violet. She's obviously not told them whose kitchen this really is. She shrugs awkwardly.

'We need to get a few ground rules straight.' I gesture to the table where I've set out some mugs and glasses. The kettle is boiled, and I've also made a jug of squash. Alison and Violet sit down, but Gretchen leans back against the shelves of cookbooks, her arms crossed.

I'm not quite sure what to do next: sit or stand; pour drinks or not. There's a strong current of tension in the room. I continue standing at the head of the table and just keep talking.

'First of all,' I say, 'secret means secret.' I look squarely at Gretchen.

She lifts her chin like I've insulted her, staring right back. 'We won't tell anyone at school,' she says. 'If that's what you're worried about.'

'Or my mum?' I realize that I've given away my entire hand in three words, but what else can I do?

She pauses long enough to make me sweat. 'Or your mum.'

Our eyes lock for a long second. I decide that enough is enough. I sit down at the table. I'm not sure which one of us has 'won', but the tension begins to ebb away. Gretchen makes herself a cup of tea and I pour squash into glasses for the rest of us.

'OK,' I say. 'That's the main thing. But there are still some other things you should know.' I look at Alison. 'Like . . . this isn't my house.'

Violet gets the cupcakes we left here out of the fridge while I explain about Mrs Simpson.

Gretchen tries not to act surprised, but I'm sure I see a new respect dawning in her eyes. I tell them about my breaking and entering to feed the cat, and how Violet and I visited Mrs Simpson in hospital.

When I'm finished, I expect some kind of reaction – questions, or something. But by then, we're all biting into the delicious pink cakes with buttercream swirls, and no one says much of anything at all. Finally, Alison wipes her mouth. 'You can trust us, Scarlett. I mean, the whole thing is cool because it's a secret.'

'And since we're a club,' Gretchen says, 'we should have some kind of secret handshake or password.'

'OK,' I acknowledge.

'How about "Banoffee"?' Violet suggests.

Gretchen makes a face.

'Maybe not.' Alison laughs.

'What about "Marzipan"?' Violet tries again.

'Too complicated,' Gretchen says.

'"Buttercream",' I say quietly.

'What's that?'

'"Buttercream".'

Gretchen looks at Violet, who nods. 'Yeah,' Gretchen says. 'That sounds good.'

'Fine,' Alison says. 'Now that we've got that over with, are we going to cook something, or what? Those free samples aren't going to make themselves.'

I get up from the table and get the little marble-covered notebook from the bookstand. 'This is the recipe book we've been using,' I say. 'It's really special – at least, I think so.'

Violet nods.

I hand it to Gretchen like a flag of truce. 'What do you guys fancy making?'

Gretchen and Alison flip through the book. 'I can't believe someone took so much time to write all of this,' Alison says. 'And the pictures – they're so cute! Let's try "The Knave of Hearts Strawberry Tarts".'

'I'd rather do "Hansel and Gretel's Gingerbread",' Gretchen says. She lowers her voice like someone might leak her preference to the PTA. 'Gingerbread is my favourite.'

Leaving them to it, I check what's in the cupboards and the fridge. To my surprise – why am I surprised by anything that happens in Rosemary's Kitchen? – there's loads of fresh fruit in the fridge, including cartons of strawberries and blueberries, kiwis, and even a punnet of cherries.

'I think we should start with fruit tarts,' I say. 'We can do gingerbread next time.' I glance at Gretchen to make sure she's OK with that.

'Fine,' she shrugs. 'Whatever.'

I take the fruit out of the fridge. Violet looks surprised too – but like me, she just goes with it.

'OK,' I say, 'now, first, everyone wash their hands. Then, someone needs to wash and cut the fruit, someone needs to make the custard, and someone needs to make the pastry for the tarts – and oh yeah, before I forget, we need to preheat the oven.'

The tasks get easily assigned. I team up with Gretchen to make the pastry dough. Together we find the ingredients and weigh them out into a bowl.

'Did your mum teach you to cook?' Gretchen asks me.

'No,' I say. 'She doesn't cook at all really. She doesn't have time.'

Gretchen stiffens and I wonder what I've said.

'I mean, she's too busy slagging me off,' I add.

She stops measuring. 'I never really got why you were so angry. Your mum made you into a star.' She frowns. 'And then, you completely changed. It was like you didn't have time for any of your friends, or anything at school any more.'

'That's totally not it.' How could Gretchen, of all people, get things so wrong?

'Well, what then?'

I tip the flour into the bowl. 'You know, before she started, I thought I was pretty normal. I sometimes did stuff I wasn't proud of . . . you know . . . embarrassing stuff. But it didn't seem like a big deal. But then, Mum started broadcasting everything. It was front page news that I passed wind at Christmas dinner and scratched my eczema in my sleep. And she'd go on about what knickers I wore, and what my gym kit smelt like. Suddenly, all that stuff seemed huge – it was all I could think about. I felt like everyone was looking at me and laughing.' I shove the bowl towards Gretchen. 'I mean, do you really think that makes me a star? Do you think I didn't have time for any of my friends so I could get more of that?'

Gretchen shrugs. 'To be honest, I didn't know what to think. I mean, you totally helped out on my campaign, and then you disappeared as soon as I won. I thought maybe you were jealous – but then, why didn't you just run yourself? You totally could have won.'

'Me?'

'I mean, you were cool – smart and talkative and stuff. Everybody thought so.'

'I thought I was "the most boring girl in the world" – your words, not mine.'

'Come on, Scarlett, I didn't really mean that. I was fed up, that's all. You never even said "congratulations" when I won. I had no idea what I'd done wrong.'

'Well, emailing my mum didn't help.'

Gretchen puts her hands on her hips. 'I thought your mum was totally cool when she started that blog. And for the record, she emailed me, not the other way around. I am the PTA rep after all. She asked me stuff about you because you stopped talking to her. I assumed she was just worried. I said maybe you weren't feeling well because it was your time of the month or something. I had no idea she was going to start writing about it.'

'So it was all a misunderstanding?'

'Maybe.'

I add the cubed butter and stir it in. I stop waiting for an apology that isn't going to come, and wonder if maybe I should be the one to say sorry. Maybe I was a little quick to drop her as a friend – just the way Stacie did to me. Maybe I should have tried to tell her how I felt six months ago. Maybe, maybe. But *maybe* it isn't too late.

I stand back and let Gretchen rub the butter into the flour. 'I'm glad you won the election,' I say. 'And I'm glad you're here now.'

'Yeah,' she says.

'It's just – the mum stuff has been awful for me. Before the blog, I guess Mum and I did get on – or at least, we were kind of normal. But now, it's *Help! My daughter this*; and *Psst! My daughter that*. All I know is – she can't find out about this.'

'She won't find out from me.' Gretchen pauses for a long second. 'I promise.'

'OK.' I hope I'm not crazy to believe her.

I close my eyes and take a bite of fruit tart. My tongue tingles at the different tastes: the pastry light and crumbly, the custard rich and wobbly, and the fruit shiny and fresh (arranged neatly by Violet) on top and covered in a sticky apricot glaze. By the time we finish up for the evening, the four of us just seem kind of normal together. I have to admit that four people seem like more of a real club than just Violet and me. I'm relieved when Gretchen volunteers to put the fruit tarts in the canteen at lunchtime. ('Well, no one will think *I'm* involved, will they?')

Once the fruit tarts have been put away, Violet, Gretchen and I clean up the kitchen (Alison manages to spend most of the clean-up time answering texts on her mobile). We double-check that we've left no trace that we were ever here, and when it's time to leave I lock the door and replace the key under the mat. Then we all repeat the secret password: 'Buttercream'.

23

TOO GOOD TO BE TRUE

Things just can't be going this well. I mean, this is my life after all. The next day, everything proceeds without a hitch. Gretchen and Alison say 'hi' to me in the hallway, but that's it – acting friendly but not too friendly. Violet smiles at me from across the room as usual. Gretchen volunteers to help the teacher photocopy something, so she doesn't even need the loo pass. And in the canteen at lunchtime, there are no fights or vomiting. Everyone queues up and gets their piece of fruit tart, and makes 'mmm-ing' noises and whispers how awesome it is, and how cool The Secret Cooking Club is. Best of all, Nick Farr still seems to be a fan. I join the queue for a slice of fruit tart, and overhear him saying something to Gretchen. 'You know, I wish I knew how to cook stuff like this.'

For a split second, I have a little fantasy – that all the noise in the room hushes up and everything goes into slow motion. All of a sudden, the universe is just me and him. I walk up boldly, tap him on the shoulder, and say, 'Why don't you join us?'

But of course, I don't.

Instead, I just try to be happy that Nick Farr and everyone else seems to like the fruit tarts and respect the club that Violet and I started, even if they'll never know I'm involved. Or so I hope, anyway.

Because when lunch is over and things are back to normal, I'm aware of a nagging feeling in the pit of my stomach that won't go away. To quote one of my mum's favourite sayings in her blog: 'Things that seem too good to be true usually are.'

After school, the four of us meet up at Mrs Simpson's house. We all say the password 'Buttercream' on our way in, giggling a little at how silly it is to have a password. Everything is the same as when we left it the previous night. Gretchen and Violet are chatting about how much everyone liked the tarts. Alison gets the little recipe book off its stand and starts flipping through it to see what we can cook today.

I go out of the kitchen to lock the front door – I'd forgotten to do it when we came in. A van is idling outside. I can't see anything through the stained-glass panel in the door, but I have the same strange feeling that I had earlier – this can't last. My heart thuds in my chest.

The others are laughing and talking loudly in the kitchen. I'm about to go and re-join them when I hear a voice outside the door. 'You sure you can manage until the nurse comes tomorrow? I'm happy to help you inside.'

And then the shrill reply of a woman's voice. 'Nonsense. I don't need anyone to help me do anything now I'm home. You can send your nurse if you like, but I won't let her in!' A key turns in the lock.

I stand there, paralysed. The door opens and I'm face to face with an old woman: Rosemary Simpson.

She takes one look at me and lets out a strangled cry of surprise.

'Mrs Simpson, please – it's OK!' I rush forward and try to help her inside. Her hair is like wire escaping from a bun at her neck and she's leaning heavily on a cane.

'Who are you? What are you doing here?' She holds up the cane with a gnarled hand and waves it at me. 'Shoo . . .'

I step back to avoid the random swing and hold up my hands. I'm aware of the others just behind me, peeking out of the kitchen door. 'I'm Scarlett,' I blurt out. 'Your neighbour. I uh . . . I've been feeding your cat.'

Her eyes are bloodshot and wild. 'Treacle? Where's Treacle? What have you done with him?'

'Nothing,' I say. 'The cat – Treacle? – hasn't been here the last few days. But I came over to check if it – he – is back.'

'Treacle?' she calls out, craning her neck to look for him.

'He isn't here.'

She whirls back on me. I cower another few steps backwards.

Violet comes up to my side. 'Hi, Mrs Simpson,' she says, 'would you like a cup of tea? We've got cupcakes left over from my birthday too. With buttercream icing and sparkles. They're really nice.'

The old lady blinks and leans forward. Her wrinkled face goes white almost like she's seen a ghost. 'Cupcakes?' she says. 'Buttercream?' She stares at the room around her like she's trying to place where she is. Her eyes settle on Violet. 'Yes,

I'll try one.' She hobbles towards the kitchen. 'And tea with two sugars and a dollop of milk.'

Gretchen and Alison make a quick retreat and start setting out cups and the last of the cupcakes on a plate. Violet sticks close to Mrs Simpson's side, pulling up a chair for her.

Alison puts the plate of cupcakes in front of the old lady, and Gretchen makes her a cup of tea. I stand well back out of the way. It's like the four of us are all holding our breath. Mrs Simpson lifts the cupcake in her trembling fingers, holds it to her nose and sniffs it. She peers closely at the icing swirls, the pink glitter, and the flower made of crystallized violets and rose petals in the centre. For a moment, she frowns. Then she takes a bite.

It seems to take for ever as she chews the cake with a clack of false teeth, and then swallows. I feel like I'm on national television awaiting the all-important verdict of the judges on *Bake Off*. Using her cane as a pivot, she swivels around in her chair and looks straight at me.

'You,' she says, pointing a wizened finger. 'You did this?'

My mouth goes dry as I try to speak. 'You're right, Mrs Simpson, I started this. We shouldn't be here – I know that. And I'm sorry. We'll leave now and never come back. Or – you can call my mum if you want. Please don't get my friends in trouble. It's all my fault, not theirs.'

'No,' Violet says, 'that's not true. We all did it. It's all of our faults.'

'Hush!' Mrs Simpson doesn't turn around, but keeps staring at me. 'This tastes like it has two teaspoons of baking powder in it. It should only have one. Don't they teach you girls any maths these days?'

'Um . . . I thought I put in one,' Gretchen says. 'I must have made a mistake.'

'And the buttercream is too solid.' She turns to Violet. 'You should have used a dash more milk. And a hint of vanilla, I think.' She licks her wrinkled lips. 'Other than that . . . it's passable.'

'Passable?'

She turns away from me back to the others. 'You've shown that you can follow a recipe.' Her voice takes on a lecturing tone. 'You can stir things together, put it in a tin and stick it in the oven.' She tsks. 'And by the way, the flapjacks you brought me were under-baked in the middle. You should have cooked them longer at a lower heat.' Her hawk-like gaze turns to Violet. 'And the crystallized violets were an interesting twist, but they made the whole thing too sweet. The bottom line is – you've found my kitchen and had your fun experimenting with your puddings and sweets.

But now . . .' She crosses her arms.

The word seems to echo around the room.

I bite my lip. She's going to tell us to leave—

'. . . now, you need to learn how to cook.'

STICK TO THE RIBS

I start to understand that old expression 'slaving over a hot stove'. Gone are the cupcakes and banoffee pie; the flapjacks and fruit tarts are a dim and distant memory. Mrs Simpson says we need to learn how to cook, and she isn't kidding.

'You can't think you know how to cook just because you can whip up a few puddings.' She peers at each of us, her sunken blue eyes twinkling. 'You girls these days are too skinny. In my day, we had rationing.' She shakes her head like the memory hurts. 'There was no sugar and no sweets. We all learnt how to cook food that "sticks to the ribs".'

I nod politely. Suddenly, I'm very hungry for real food.

She flips the pages of the notebook, pausing and considering.

'Do you know what I craved most as a girl after the war?' Mrs Simpson says, her bushy eyebrows raised.

We shake our heads.

'Eggs. That's what. Real eggs, perfectly cooked, and everything that goes with them. But all we had back then were powdered eggs. You don't know how lucky you are.' She purses her lips. 'Now I use only the freshest of ingredients – that's one of the secrets of being a good cook.'

'Is that the secret ingredient?' I ask shyly.

'No.' My question seems to startle her. 'Not that.' Her eyes suddenly appear glassy and far away. 'That's something else entirely.'

For a long moment I worry that I've spoilt everything. I look down at the floor, scarcely daring to breathe.

'So we'll start with this one.' Recovering, she props open the recipe book on the stand. Relief flows through me. The recipe on the page is for 'Chicken Licken's Eggs Benedict'. 'If you can't cook an egg properly, then you may as well get out of the kitchen.'

*

The four of us go through a whole dozen eggs, cracking them into cups, before Mrs Simpson is even halfway satisfied with our egg-breaking technique. Even Gretchen is sweating by the time we end up with a load of eggs in cups ready to poach. Mrs Simpson assigns Gretchen to do the poaching and prepare the sliced ham, Violet and Alison to bake the muffins, and me to make the hollandaise sauce.

While Mrs Simpson is helping Gretchen get the equipment out of the cupboards, I turn to Violet. 'Looks like we have another new member.'

'It's all a little weird, isn't it?' Violet keeps her voice low.

'What?'

'That she'd just let us stay and carry on cooking.'

I shrug. 'Maybe it was the flapjacks.'

'Or she's just lonely,' Alison says. Flour puffs everywhere as she tips it into the bowl.

'Anyway,' I say, 'let's just go with it for now.'

It's like we're under a spell. An hour goes by, then another. Nothing else seems to matter – if we're expected at home, or have homework or had other plans. The muffins bake, the hollandaise sauce gets whisked up and made. Mrs Simpson tells us stories about how people cooked during the war, and about how when she was a girl, they didn't have Tesco or microwave ready meals or anything like that. While she mostly lets us get on with following the recipe, occasionally she cackles the odd instruction, or bangs her stick against the floor to make a point. The four of us scurry around like old-time kitchen maids.

Somehow we manage to finish making the Eggs Benedict. My stomach is rumbling because it's almost eight o'clock and none of us have eaten anything. Violet stacks everything on the plates: muffin, ham, egg and a little swirl of hollandaise sauce for decoration. The four of us sneak glances at each other as Mrs Simpson sits down at the table and cuts a piece of what we've made. I think we're all holding our breath – I know I am.

She raises the fork to her lips and pops the bite-ful into her mouth. She chews slowly and deliberately, the skin on her neck wobbling as she finally swallows it down.

Then she looks up. 'Well,' she says, waving an exasperated hand. 'Don't just stand there gawping. Sit down and eat.'

The other three scramble to sit down at the table, but I stand there, my hands on my hips. 'But aren't you going to say if it's any good?'

She looks up at me slowly, still chewing. She

pats her lips with a napkin, and takes a sip of tea.

'You cooked it,' she says. 'Only you can say for sure.'

'Oh,' I say, not really understanding.

I sit down at the table. My friends and I silently lift our knives and forks, like taking the first bite is some kind of test. I cut a piece off the little tower of eggs and muffin and stick it in my mouth. The tastes are wholesome and familiar, yet new at the same time. It strikes me that I've never before really paid attention to what I eat – the different flavours and textures. Maybe part of learning how to cook is learning how to eat. I look up and notice that Mrs Simpson is watching *me* chew the first bite. Her lips pursed in a thin line, she nods almost imperceptibly at me. I smile down at my plate. I know it's good.

In no time at all, everyone's plate is completely empty. My only regret is that we didn't make more. 'Shall we start the washing-up?' I ask Mrs Simpson.

'First let's talk about what we cooked tonight, and what we learnt.'

She goes around the table, asking each of us in turn what we thought of the dish we made. Alison says that it tasted 'good', and Violet says that it was 'fun to make'. But Mrs Simpson keeps questioning us, making us talk about things like the balance of the seasoning, the texture of the eggs, the crispiness of the muffins. Gretchen thought that the sauce was a little runny; Violet thought that her muffin was too brown on the bottom. When it gets to be my turn, I don't quite know what to say.

'I thought that everything we used went really well together,' I muster finally. 'Like it belonged that way all along.'

For the first time all evening, Mrs Simpson manages a little smile. The years melt off her face. I smile back, glad to have given a 'right' answer. 'In that case,' she says, 'I think we're done here. Now, off with you – I want this kitchen sparkling before you leave.'

'Yes, Mrs Simpson,' we all say in unison.

We jump up from the table and start a marathon of washing up dishes, cleaning surfaces, putting away ingredients and wiping down the hob. I keep stealing glances at Mrs Simpson as she drinks another cup of tea, wondering about her. Tonight she's made me think about cooking in a whole new way. And I feel good inside about what I've accomplished. That's the best part.

But by the time I finish drying the dishes, Mrs Simpson's eyes are closed and her head is drooping. Her grip loosens on her stick, and it falls to the floor with a thud.

'We have to get her to bed,' I say. We take off our aprons and help Mrs Simpson to the sofa in the front room. We cover her with an orange knitted throw. Less than a minute later, she's asleep. All of a sudden I realize how irresponsible we've been – it must have been a shock for her to come home from hospital only to find a cooking club in her kitchen. We should have left hours ago.

'Can we just leave her?' I say to Gretchen. Together we unfasten the old lady's shoes.

'I'm not sure we have much choice. I guess she'll be OK if she's asleep.'

'Uh oh!' Alison looks at the screen of her phone for the first time all evening. 'I told my mum that I'd be home by half eight from your house, Gretch. And now it's almost half nine. And I was supposed to finish that stupid essay.'

Gretchen shrugs. 'We're all in the same boat.'

'Where's her stick?' I say. 'She'll need it when she wakes up.'

'Still in the kitchen, I guess,' Violet says.

'I'll just go and get it.'

I go back to the kitchen. The little recipe notebook is closed on the rack, like it's resting for the night. The plates and dishes that we used have been washed and are drying on the draining board of the sink. The pots and pans are drying at the back of the hob. There's a faint hissing sound like a tap is running somewhere. I check the kitchen tap – it's off. One of the wet tea towels is crumpled up on the counter. I hang it up over the front of the range to dry faster. I pick up Mrs Simpson's stick and take it into the front room, propping it against the sofa so she can't miss it.

'Let's go,' I say. 'I'll come back tomorrow morning and check that she's OK.'

We all grab our school bags and head out of the door. We're in such a hurry that no one even thinks to give the secret password.

Maybe that's what we did wrong.

25

KETCHUP SKY

There's a light on under the door to the Mum Cave when I get back home. I tiptoe out of the kitchen towards the stairs when all of a sudden Mum bursts out.

'Scarlett! Where have you been? I've been so worried.' She engulfs me in her special stale-smelling Mum hug. 'I was about to call the police. I can't believe you did this to me *again*.'

I'm so tired that I just stand there letting her squeeze me.

'Sorry, Mum,' I say. 'But I did tell you about the science project. We're working in pairs to build' – I scratch my head, trying to remember what we've done in science class this year – 'a solar-powered car.'

'Really?' Mum looks disappointed – she won't get much mileage out of that in her blog.

'I'm paired up with a new girl. Her name is Violet.'

Mum steps back. I have to catch myself from slumping. 'All right, maybe you did mention it before – I don't remember.' She shrugs dismissively. 'But I think it's time we got you a phone. Just so you can let me know where you are.'

'A phone? Really?' Mum's always been opposed to girls my age having phones or tablets – anything like that. While I've got her old laptop computer and printer to do my homework, she won't even let me have internet access. She's already done a post on: *We didn't have any of that stuff in my day . . . so you don't need it either*. 'That would be great.'

'I really was worried, Scarlett. I hope you know that.'

I nod, wishing I could say more – tell her that I'm grateful that she was worried about me. But the words won't come out.

'It's just, there's something strange with this house sometimes.' She stares at the wall, oddly distracted. 'It's like, I keep smelling things. And remembering . . .'

'Really?' I say. 'Like what?'

'Never mind.' She shakes her head. 'I've got to get back to work now.' She goes to her office door. 'And because you gave me a fright, you're grounded.'

Grounded! I try to protest, but she slams the door of the Mum Cave in my face. This is the first time she's ever grounded me, and I can just imagine her sitting gleefully at her computer and typing up a new blog entry: *A Mum's Pop Quiz: how many years has my daughter taken off my life?*

But as long as she doesn't know about The Secret Cooking Club, I can live with whatever rubbish she writes. I realize that since we started the club, I'm stronger somehow; more confident. More like my old self.

I go upstairs and brush my teeth. I can't remember ever being so happy to flop into my own bed. I pull the duvet up to my neck and close my eyes. But sleep doesn't come. I go back over the events of the night: from Rosemary Simpson's surprise arrival, to the egg dish that we made, to how full my stomach feels having eaten something fresh and healthy. But there's a little niggle at the back of my mind that won't go away. A hissing sound – like a tap is running somewhere . . .

'Wake up, Scarlett!'

A hand is shaking me in the dark. There's a

strange reddish orange glow outside the net curtains, and something smells funny.

'The sky is ketchup,' Kelsie says. She pulls the duvet off me. 'Come and see.'

I swing out of bed with a sleepy groan. The blood rushes from my head. Something is very wrong.

'Girls!' Mum's voice is frantic as she runs up the stairs. 'We need to get outside right now. Something's burning.'

Burning!

All of a sudden I hear the scream of a siren rushing down the road. The ketchup sky begins to flash with the glow of the spinning dome on the fire engine.

'Mrs Simpson!' I cry. 'She's in there.'

'Who?' Mum barks.

'Our neighbour! She's just come home from hospital.'

We rush outside the front door. A small crowd of neighbours has gathered across the road.

Firefighters pour out of the shiny red truck – there's at least six of them – and go up to Mrs Simpson's front door. One of them tries the door and another one gets ready to bash it in.

'There's a key underneath the mat,' I yell, rushing forwards. 'You don't need to bust down the door.'

One of the firefighters gets the key and unlocks the door.

'Please step back,' another one says to me. 'Across the road at the very least.'

'Scarlett?' Mum's voice warns. 'Come away now.' She pulls me along by the arm, her other hand herding Kelsie. When we're across the road I turn back, petrified, as the fireman pushes open the door. But there's no billowing cloud of smoke: just an old lady's frightened cry: 'Who are you, young man? Go away now. Shoo . . .'

Two more firefighters dash in, one carrying a full-length stretcher. Mrs Simpson's protests grow even louder. 'This is my house – and I'm not leaving!'

The remaining firefighters go inside, dragging along a limp fire hose. I hear a loud crash of glass. 'Please, lady!' A man's voice. 'We're trying to help you. There's a fire in your kitchen.'

Mum is busy trying to get Kelsie to take her thumb out of her mouth. Sensing my chance, I dash back across the road. One of the neighbours calls out, and then Mum yells, 'Stop, Scarlett,' but I keep going. Mrs Simpson knows me – I can help get her out of the burning house.

But just as my foot hits the kerb, a sleek black Mercedes pulls up. I stop. A man jumps out of the car: tall with a high forehead, thin nose and slicked-back dark hair. He's wearing a smart black suit and shiny black shoes. He turns to the crowd and waves briefly. Then he strides past me and up to the door.

'Aunt Rosemary?' he calls out loudly. Water begins to whoosh through the hosepipe.

'No!' Mrs Simpson's voice. 'Turn off that water right now!'

I realize that Mr Black Mercedes must be the nephew, Mr Kruffs. Somehow, I'd pictured him as different – shorter, stouter, more like a fluffy poodle at Crufts dog show. But this man looks more like a slick, modern version of the Child Snatcher. Not someone I'd like to cross.

A moment later, the two firefighters come outside with Mrs Simpson between them – kicking and dragging her feet like a criminal resisting arrest. Mr Kruffs makes a big show of trying to take his aunt's arm. He waves to the crowd that everything's OK – obviously playing up the 'politician-rescues-old-lady-from-burning-building' angle. Several people take pictures with their phones.

Mrs Simpson jerks her arm away. 'You can go now, Emory,' she says. 'Everything is fine.'

'Fine?' His voice is low. 'Your house is burning down – with you in it.'

'Well . . .' Mrs Simpson yanks her stick away

from one of the firemen, 'this lot has everything sorted. And it was only a very *small* fire . . .' She turns to the crowd across the street and waves her cane. 'Go away – shoo . . .'

I step forward. 'Mrs Simpson?' I try to sound calm and soothing. 'Are you OK? Can I help?'

Mr Kruffs gives me an intense glare down his long nose, like I've just thrown an egg at his car. 'Who are you?'

I stand my ground. 'I'm her neighbour.'

'Well, go back across the road, please. It's not safe for kids here.'

Mrs Simpson stares at me with pleading blue eyes. 'Scarlett?' she says, sounding confused.

'That's right, Mrs Simpson.' Ignoring Mr Kruffs, I reach forward and take her arm gently. 'Shall we go and wait across the road until this is over?'

The old woman looks at her nephew, hesitating. Before she can make up her mind, one of the firemen comes out.

'Everything is under control,' he says, loud enough for the crowd to hear. 'You can all go back to bed.'

Someone chuckles like he's said something funny. No one leaves. I glance over at Mum, who's talking to a woman from down the street. I catch a snippet about Boots and the 'Mum's Survival Kit'.

Mr Kruffs steps up and stands next to the fireman. 'Everything is going to be fine now.' He grins widely as a few more photos are snapped. 'I think we should all get out of the way now and let our brave firefighters finish doing their jobs.'

The crowd murmurs, and a few people begin to leave.

I lean closer to Mrs Simpson and listen as the fireman speaks to Mr Kruffs. 'It was just a small, contained fire,' he says. 'The hob in the kitchen was left on and a tea towel caught fire.'

'A tea towel . . .' My hand flies to my mouth. *What have I done?*

The fireman continues talking to Mr Kruffs. 'There's some smoke damage, a burnt window frame and a broken window. It could have been a lot worse.'

But things *are* worse. I know that as soon as I take a look at Mr Kruffs, his face grimacing in concern. 'The hob was left on,' he repeats. He shakes his head and tsks dramatically. 'Really, Aunt Rosemary.'

'It wasn't her fault!' I say. Guilt and fear churn inside me.

'Please stay out of this,' Mr Kruffs says sharply. He turns back to his aunt. 'This proves that you can't keep living here on your own.'

Her face crumples. 'Yes, I can,' she says. 'And

I wouldn't be on my own if you hadn't taken Treacle.'

Mr Kruffs gives a pained-looking shrug. 'Shouldn't you be thanking me for that? That greedy old cat could have starved to death while you were in hospital.'

'He's not greedy,' I cut in. 'And he wouldn't have starved. *I* was feeding him. You should bring him back.'

Mr Kruffs peers down at me like a vulture in a tall tree. 'This is nothing to do with you,' he says.

Mrs Simpson's bony hand tightens on my arm. 'It's everything to do with me,' I say with a sudden surge of protectiveness. 'Mrs Simpson is my neighbour – we share a wall. If her house had burnt down, so would ours.' I turn to the old lady. 'Come on, Mrs Simpson, let's go. I'll ask Mum if you can sleep at our house tonight.'

'There, Emory, you see?' Rosemary Simpson gives her nephew a defiant look. She allows me to steer her away. She hobbles towards our house, leaning heavily on both me and her stick.

'I'll be back in the morning,' Mr Kruffs says. In two strides he's back at the black Mercedes and getting into the driver's seat. 'We'll talk about this further. And this time, I'm going to take some action.'

Mrs Simpson's whole body starts to tremble.

'It's OK,' I whisper. 'It's going to be fine.'

'Don't let him put me in a home, please.'

'I won't, Mrs Simpson.' I bite my lip. 'I promise.'

26

MAPLE SYRUP

But how on earth can I promise something like that? I'm the one who failed to notice that the burner was still on. I'm the one who draped the tea towel too close. The fire was my fault, and Mrs Simpson is paying the price! I stand next to her, feeling like my chest might explode. All of a sudden, Mum storms across the road, pulling my sister along with her. She takes my arm and pulls me a little way away.

'Scarlett,' she scolds, 'that man is a politician. You sounded very rude when you spoke to him. What's going on?'

'Mum . . .' I choke. *Tell her. No, don't tell her. What*

should I do? I take a long breath to pull myself together. 'Please can Mrs Simpson stay at our house tonight? It sounds like the firemen have made a bit of a mess in there. She needs somewhere to go.'

Mum looks at Mrs Simpson's bent figure, then back at me. Her cheeks are red from the cold air and the effort of boring the pants off our neighbour with stories of the Boots product selection committee.

'Honestly, Scarlett!' she says in a harassed whisper. 'We can't take someone in just like that. Where would she sleep?'

'In my bed, or on the sofa bed – I don't care.'

'But we don't even know her—'

'We can't just leave her out here!' I cry. 'She's our neighbour, and her house was on fire. We need to help her.'

'But I've got a deadline – I'm so busy . . .' Mum shakes her head. 'You know that, Scarlett.'

I take a breath. 'I do know that, Mum. You have to write your blog. What's it going to be this time: *Help! My teenage daughter is taking in vagrants off the street?* Or maybe, *Psst! My thoughtless daughter made me miss my deadline*. But if you write that, I'm going to get online and be the first person to leave a comment.' I stand up straighter. 'I'm going to tell everyone – all your precious readers, Twitter followers and Facebook friends – that the old lady who lives next door had no place to go and you wouldn't even let her sleep on the sofa for one night.' I raise my chin. 'How do you think *that* will make you look at your next meeting with Boots?'

'You wouldn't dare,' Mum spits. 'If you ever do anything to hurt my reputation online, then I'll . . . I'll . . .'

'It's just for one night, Mum. Let Mrs Simpson stay with us for one night.'

Mum's eyes skewer me but I can't back down – not now. 'We're not done with this conversation.' She walks over to Mrs Simpson – the old lady seems to have dozed off leaning on her stick – and puts her hand on her arm. 'Mrs Simpson?' Mum sounds like she's talking to a child. 'I'm Claire – Scarlett's mum. If you need a place to stay for tonight, you can come next door to ours . . .'

Somehow I manage to fall asleep, because when I wake up the next morning, my body feels like lead. The memories of the night come rushing back – the fire that I caused; standing up to Mr Kruffs *and* Mum; and most of all, the helpless look of trust on Mrs Simpson's face through it all. I get out of bed and rush to the window. The fire engines are gone without any sign that they were ever really here. Everything is still and quiet. I get dressed and go downstairs to check on our guest.

The blanket is folded on the sofa and the room is empty. I feel a stab of panic. I'd offered Mrs Simpson my bed, but she said that she preferred to sleep on the sofa downstairs. What if she wandered off in the night – sleepwalking maybe – and got hit by a car? Or maybe Mr Kruffs broke in and gagged her and took her off to a home, and I'll never know where she is or what happened, and it's all my fault—

And then I smell it. Like a zombie, I turn and leave the room in a daze. Whatever it is, it's coming from *our* kitchen – and I can already tell that it's going to be delicious.

I practically collide at the bottom of the stairs with Mum. She's looks sleepy and cross with uncombed hair and no make-up.

'I'm sorry, Mum,' I blurt out. 'I shouldn't have said those things last night.'

She rubs her eyes. 'No, Scarlett, I was the one who was wrong. You were just trying to be kind and neighbourly – the way I raised you.'

I smile faintly and don't bother to contradict her.

Mum sniffs the air. 'What's that? It smells like cooking.'

'I think it's Mrs Simpson's way of saying thank you.'

Mum raises her eyebrows. 'Oh?'

I follow her to the kitchen. Mum stops at the door and gasps. A second later, I can see why.

The kitchen is immaculate – the washing-up has been done, the magazines and clutter neatly stacked to one side, and the table has been washed and set with four places. There are two large cast-iron pans on the hob, one filled with four sizzling eggs, and one that I can't see because Mrs Simpson's back is blocking my view. She's standing up straight and steady without any sign of her stick. A second later, she lifts the frying pan and something flips up into the air. She catches it in the pan and removes it with a spatula on to a plate.

'Sit down,' she says, without turning round. 'Everything will be ready in about five minutes.'

Mum and I look at each other with wide eyes. I wouldn't even think of not obeying the command. Mum sits down at one end of the table. I sit down at my usual place, and behind me I hear the shuffling feet of my sister in her bunny slippers.

'Oooh, breakfast,' Kelsie says. 'Smells nice.'

'Yeah,' I say. 'Sit down.'

Mrs Simpson brings Mum a steaming cup of coffee. 'Thank you,' Mum says in a croaky voice. The milk and sugar are already set out neatly in front of her. Mrs Simpson goes back to the hob and spoons more batter into the hot pan.

'I'm not the biggest fan of American cooking nowadays,' the old lady says. 'It's all non-fat this and no-carbs that. But when they do things the old-fashioned, home-cooked way, they get it right. Like pancakes and pure maple syrup. Nothing beats it, if you ask me.'

'I love pancakes!' my sister says. 'It's like when we went to Disney World.'

I smile at her. Just before Dad left, we had a family holiday to Florida. We stayed at a little motel next to an International House of Pancakes. I can just about remember how good everything tasted.

'Where did you get everything?' Mum asks, looking flustered. 'I'm afraid I forgot to arrange a food delivery for this week.'

'From my house,' Mrs Simpson says. 'The fire really was nothing – just a little smoke damage.' She smiles in my direction. 'The refrigerator was fine. I went over early to make sure I saved what I could.'

'Good thinking,' Mum says. 'And I'm glad the fire wasn't serious.'

'Um,' I say, biting my lip, 'there's something I need to say—'

Mrs Simpson cuts me off with a quick finger to her lips. I stop. She begins handing around the plates.

'It's just – can I help with that?' I mumble.

She waves away my offer. This is her moment.

As well as pancakes, maple syrup and perfectly cooked eggs, there's bacon, fruit salad and toast with fresh strawberry jam from a jar with a handwritten label. It's like being in breakfast heaven.

When everyone else is served, Mrs Simpson sets down her own plate, but keeps standing up behind her chair. 'Eat it while it's hot,' she says. She watches intently as we pick up our forks and try the food. After that, no one speaks – it's all too delicious for words. Mrs Simpson finally sits down, a satisfied smile on her face. I smile too – for a second. Then I'm back to eating the best breakfast ever.

Mum gracefully ducks out after a second helping – but before the washing-up – and Kelsie goes off to watch TV. I'm left facing Mrs Simpson across the table.

'That was amazing,' I say. 'Thank you so much.'

Mrs Simpson sighs and begins clearing the plates.

I jump up. 'I'll do that,' I say, taking the plate from her hand and running water in the sink to do the washing-up.

'No, child.' She waves at me to sit back down. 'I've got a headache. And when that happens, it helps to have something to focus on. I need to think straight.'

I pour myself a third glass of fresh orange juice and sit down. 'What can I do to help you?' I say. 'Violet and I – well, all of us really – we'd like to do something. Your nephew has no right to put you in a home. He just can't!'

The old lady's shoulders droop like a wilted flower.

'I mean, you didn't start that fire! We left the hob on, and I put the tea towel on the front of the cooker to dry. The fire was my fault. And I'm going to tell your nephew – and my mum – the truth.' I feel like a prisoner marching to the scaffold, but I know it's the right thing to do.

Mrs Simpson straightens up suddenly and turns to me. 'Don't mention it to them, Scarlett,' she says. 'It won't help anything. If Emory knows you were there in the house, it might make things worse.'

'But why? Isn't it worse if he thinks you can't look after yourself?'

She turns back to the sink and begins soaping the dishes with a sponge, pausing only to tuck a stray strand of grey hair back into her bun. 'Everyone gets old,' she says finally. 'There's no escaping that. I have to go some time – and I'm OK with that. I'd just like to stay in my own home as long as I can, that's all.' She stops talking. A tear runs down her cheek – or maybe it's just a soapsud.

I stand up. 'How about I dry?' I offer.

Mrs Simpson nods. I grab a tea towel and we both go about the washing-up in silence. My mind is turning over and over. There must be something that I can do – something that The Secret Cooking Club can do. But what?

When we've finished the dishes, Mrs Simpson dries her hands and takes off her apron. Her ankles are thick and saggy in too-dark nude tights.

'I'd like my cat to be with me,' she says. 'If I have to go into one of *those* places.'

'We need to get Treacle back anyway.' I fold my arms stubbornly. 'And as far as I'm concerned, you're not going anywhere if you don't want to.'

Her smile is fragile. 'Thank you, child. And now, I'd like to go back to my house.'

'Are you sure?' Part of me was hoping that Mrs Simpson would stay here with us.

'Yes,' she insists. 'I have to deal with this on my own. Trust me, it's better that way.' She rubs her temples like she's in pain.

'But what about the fire? I mean, aren't you mad at us?'

She gives a little chuckle. 'Let me tell you a secret, Scarlett. Everyone makes mistakes. In this case, there was no harm done, you learnt something, and it will never happen again. I know that.'

'Oh,' I say, some of the tension draining away. 'I'm sorry all the same.'

'I know.' She smiles.

'You'll be OK going home on your own?'

'Yes, I will.' She grips her stick tightly and hobbles towards the front door. I open it and she goes outside, her stick clonking on the pavement. I watch to make sure she's OK. When she gets to her own front door, she stops. 'By the way, Scarlett,' she says.

'Yeah? I mean . . . yes?'

'I shall expect you and your friends at five o'clock today. Don't be late.'

I stare at her in disbelief.

'Um, OK,' I say. 'We won't be.'

Back inside my house I get Mum's mobile from its charger and quickly ring Violet.

'We've got a situation,' I say. I tell her all about the fire; about Mrs Simpson staying with us; about the breakfast – and about how we can't be late.

'Oh, Scarlett,' Violet says, 'that's so awful. I can't believe that we . . . It's terrible!'

'I wanted to tell Mr Kruffs, but she didn't want me to. She said it would only make things worse. But I'm not sure I believe that. We have to do something.'

'And she really still wants us to come over? Didn't you say the whole kitchen was on fire?'

'No. Luckily it wasn't that bad – just a bit of smoke damage. It could have been a lot worse apparently. But now Mr Kruffs is trying to put her in a home.'

'A home? But she has a home.'

'No! I mean an old people's home. Like one of those awful places you hear about on the news. I bet there's nothing to do but sit around and watch TV and play bridge. You probably have to eat horrible mushy food so that your dentures don't fall out. Everyone's pretty much just waiting to die.'

'Ugh.' Violet shudders. 'She can't go there. But what can we do?'

Secretly, I'm a little disappointed that Violet doesn't have a solution – because I know I don't.

'Can you call Gretchen and Alison?' I grasp at straws. 'We need an emergency meeting right after school. We have to think of something.'

BRAINSTORMING

When The Secret Cooking Club gathers in the front room of Violet's aunt's house, everyone starts talking at once. 'Who used the hob last?' Gretchen tries to get to the bottom of things.

'I don't know,' Violet says. 'Maybe me, or Alison, I don't remember—'

'I'm sure I checked,' Alison wails. 'It wasn't me.'

'Look,' I hold up my hand. 'This won't help. We're a club, so in some ways we're all responsible.' I swallow hard. 'Besides, I went into the kitchen last—'

'You're right – it doesn't matter,' Gretchen says. 'It happened and we need to move on – together.'

Everyone nods glumly. I pass around a bowl of tasteless cheese crisps.

'We could meet here sometimes,' Violet volunteers. 'As long as we clean up really well. Aunt Hilda doesn't cook, and she doesn't like the smell of food in the kitchen.'

'What good is a kitchen where you can't cook?' Gretchen says stroppily.

'We could meet at my house,' Alison says. 'Mum doesn't get home from work until seven. She doesn't cook either, but she's got a lot of stuff we could use.'

I shake my head. 'That's not the point. Even if we could find somewhere else, it won't be the same.'

'I agree,' Violet says. 'Besides, we've made things worse for Mrs Simpson: her nephew's threatening to send her to an old people's home because she can't look after herself. We can't just leave her to be locked away eating mushy food until she dies.'

'Mushy food?' Alison looks horrified. 'She'd hate that.'

I clear my throat to get things back on track. 'And anyway,' I say, 'she's teaching us. I've never had a mentor before.'

'Me neither,' Gretchen says. 'And I guess she must have enjoyed it too if she wants us to come back. So what do we do?'

'Well, I was kind of hoping you might have some ideas,' I say. 'Since you're involved in the PTA and all that.'

Gretchen gives me an exasperated look. 'Have you ever been to a PTA meeting?'

'No.'

She shakes her head. 'Forget it.'

'I have an idea.' Alison flicks a lock of blonde hair out of her eyes. The three of us turn towards her. I stifle a mean little thought that it's probably the first time she's ever spoken those words. 'Well, I *do*.' Alison glares at Gretchen (who must have been thinking the same as me). 'I was thinking that maybe we could have a bake-a-thon or something.'

I sit back in my chair. 'Go on . . .'

'I don't know. Maybe we could get sponsors and advertisers, and people could make pledges to a PayPal account. Nick says you can raise money by doing stuff online. I mean . . . look at your mum.' She glances sideways at me like she's still trying to figure out why I deserve to have a 'celebrity' in the family.

The mention of Nick Farr makes my cheeks go hot. 'Well, I don't know anything about what Mum does, other than make my life miserable,' I say. 'Besides, even if we raised money, what good would that do?'

'Mrs Simpson could hire a nurse or carer,' Gretchen says. 'That's what happened when my gran got really old. The carer came in once a day at first. At the end, she was there round the clock.'

'It's definitely something to consider, I guess.'

'But what about Mr Kruffs?' Violet says. She lowers her voice. 'Aunt Hilda said that he's keen to have Mrs Simpson sell her house. I think he owns a share of it or something. Maybe that's why he's so keen to get rid of her.'

'That's pretty low,' Gretchen says.

'You know,' I say, 'there is one thing that we might be able to do – about Mr Kruffs, if he causes trouble.'

'What's that?' Violet asks.

'Well . . .' I think aloud. 'I know how stressed my mum gets over her "online image" and the number of Facebook friends and Twitter followers that she has. She's always going on about it.'

'She's got loads, hasn't she?' Gretchen says admiringly.

'But she's always trying to get more. And if Mr Kruffs is running for MP, he's probably worried about his public image too.'

'The "grey vote"!' Gretchen says. 'That's what you call it when you want old people to vote for you.'

'Yeah. And it wouldn't look very good if everyone knew that he put his aunt in a home, would it?'

'No!' Violet's eyes blaze. 'I wouldn't vote for him. No way.'

'So if he tries anything, we expose him.'

'OK,' Gretchen says. 'It's a start. And now, we'd better head over to her house.'

'Yeah.' Alison stands up quickly. 'I'm starving and I want to cook something, not sit around here.' She eyes the bowl of cheese crisps disdainfully.

'Me too.' I stand up while Violet tosses the rest of the crisps in the bin. 'Let's go.'

We go to Mrs Simpson's house and ring the bell. There's no outward sign that there ever was a fire, or that anyone is home. Or whether or not Mr Kruffs came around as promised. After a minute there's no answer so I knock hard on the door. A wave of anxiety rises inside me.

'Is the key still there?' Violet says. 'We ought to at least check that she's OK.'

I bend down and check under the mat. The key is there as usual. I unlock the door and we all go inside. There's a smell of smoke, and the house is quiet like it's holding its breath. I tiptoe towards the light under the kitchen door, feeling nervous.

As I'm about to turn the knob, a voice comes from inside. 'You're two minutes late.'

Mrs Simpson's voice.

I open the door. Part of the wall is charred black, the window is blocked with cardboard, and there are towels on the floor mopping up the last of the water. Mrs Simpson's copper kettle is on the hob with steam coming out of it – at least the stove seems to be working. I suck in a breath through my teeth, feeling guilty all over again.

Mrs Simpson looks up from where she's sitting at the table, cookbooks spread out before her. There's also a piece of paper and a pen.

'I'm sorry we're late,' I say. 'And just so you know, we all wanted to say—'

She holds up her hand to silence me.

'You wanted to say that you're sorry, and that it won't happen again. I know all that, so let's just skip it and get down to business.' She lifts her chin proudly.

'Yes, Mrs Simpson,' we all say in unison.

'I've made up a menu.' She holds up the piece of paper. Four of you, and four courses. Sound fair enough?'

OMG!

For the next few hours, I forget about the fire, my problems, Mrs Simpson's problems, and everything else – except trying to cook something special that meets her high standards.

AN IDEA

At school the next day I daydream about the evening at Mrs Simpson's house. For the first time ever, I ate like I was in a five-star restaurant. There was French onion soup with home-grown herbs; spicy crab cakes with a dill mayonnaise; perfectly marinated rib-eye steaks with tender vegetables; and for pudding, my own special creation – a mint and strawberry chocolate soufflé.

Mrs Simpson didn't even lift a spoon during the cooking process, but she hovered over each step; approving the measuring and mixing of ingredients like she was four people at once. She also set the table with fine gold-rimmed china, snow-white linen placemats and napkins, and gold and silver candles. We didn't talk about the fire, or her worries, or any of our own.

Once, as we were cooking, I'd tried to ask her about the little recipe book hoping she'd tell us more about the dedication – 'To my Little Cook – may you find the secret ingredient.' 'It's a really lovely little book,' I'd said. 'It must have taken you ages to make.'

But Mrs Simpson didn't answer right away. Her breathing seemed to grow shallow and I could tell that I'd upset her. But a moment later, she'd recovered. 'It was a long time ago,' she'd said, her hand trembling as she raised a teacup to her lips. I'd taken the hint – and Violet had helpfully asked a question about how long to cook the vegetables in order to change the subject.

When dinner was served, Mrs Simpson got us each talking about the good bits about ourselves: our happiest times, our best memories, what we want to be when we grow up – stuff that might seem lame, but actually was nice to talk about.

Gretchen talked a lot about her family and how close they are. I already knew her dad is a barrister, but I didn't know that her mum is the head of HR for some bank. Or that she has an older brother who works for a clean water charity in Africa. No wonder Gretchen tries hard to be Ms Perfect. And succeeds – most of the time, at least. 'I want to study law like my dad,' she said proudly. 'So I can help people with their problems. But I'll need to know how to cook for when I'm at university. And, you know, after.'

Alison acted unusually shy when Mrs Simpson asked her about her future ambitions. Before answering, she looked at Gretchen as if seeking permission. 'I wanted to go to ballet school,' she told us, 'but I had to have an operation on my knee. So that's not going to be possible now.'

I saw her through new eyes, feeling surprised and sympathetic. Alison has turned out to be nicer than I expected, but I didn't know that she'd had that happen to her.

'But I'm kind of OK with it,' she continued. 'I was thinking that I could start a dance studio someday. I like working with kids. But who knows . . .' She smiled in my direction. 'Maybe I'll teach cooking too so that girls who want to be dancers can still eat healthily. It's really fun – I never would have guessed.'

Mrs Simpson nodded thoughtfully. 'The best way to eat healthily is to use healthy ingredients – vegetables, nuts, fruits, fish – all as fresh as possible. I've got some special recipes I can show you.'

'Great,' Alison said. 'I'd like that.'

When Mrs Simpson turned to Violet and asked her what she wanted to be, Violet surprised everyone except me by saying that she wants to be a doctor. 'I want to save lives,' she said. Her eyes flicked over to me, but she didn't tell the rest of them what she had told me. 'But until I can do that, I'm happy enough baking things. I was really scared to come to a new school,' she admitted. 'But now that we've got The Secret Cooking Club, I'm glad I did.'

'Yeah,' I said. 'The Secret Cooking Club has been good for all of us.'

'And what about you, Scarlett?' Mrs Simpson asked.

I'd been waiting for the question, and made up all kinds of answers in my mind: like winning *Bake Off*, writing my own cookbook, or helping end hunger in Africa. But instead, I decided to answer truthfully.

'I don't know, really,' I said. 'I'm kind of just trying to enjoy what I've got now – like you guys.'

'Let's toast the Secret Cooking Club,' Violet replied raising her glass.

'To Mrs Simpson,' I said.

'To mixing friends and flour,' Gretchen added.

'To buttercream,' Alison laughed.

Mrs Simpson leant forwards. 'To friendship,'

she said.

'Hear, hear.'

The kitchen echoed with the tinkling of crystal as we all clinked our glasses together. And even though it took a long time to wash and put away all that fine china, it was a really good night.

But now . . .

'Hey Scarlett, wait up!'

I turn round and see that the person trying to get my attention is Nick Farr. I feel like everything I ate for breakfast might come up again. Alison and Gretchen are good friends with Nick, so why does talking to a boy make me so nervous?

'Oh, hi.' I stop walking and turn, feeling myself blush.

'Alison said you needed some help – with an online profile or something?'

'Um, I do—?'

'That's what she said.' His cute-as-a-boy-band-member face slips into a frown.

Get a grip, Scarlett! 'I mean – yes, I do.'

He raises an eyebrow. 'I've got my laptop in my bag. I can meet you in the library after school. But I don't have long. I'm helping coach a junior rugby team later tonight.'

'Oh.'

'OK, well . . .' He gives me a look like he's sorry he bothered to speak to me in the first place. 'I'll see you later then?'

'Yeah. Thanks.'

I make a dash for the girls' loos. My insides feel liquid and gushy. *Nick Farr spoke to me. Nick Farr is going to meet me after school. OMG! I am going to die/be sick/fall down on my knees and thank Alison/kill Alison/run screaming from the building/go home and change my clothes/wash my hair/take a cold shower/crawl under the duvet and never come out.*

'So did Nick talk to you?' Violet emerges from the far cubicle, smiling mischievously.

'You're in on it too! I thought I was going to die.'

'Come on, Scarlett,' she laughs. 'This is your big chance.'

'For what!'

She cocks her head like I'm stupid or something. 'We agreed it, I thought. If we're online we might be able to raise money to help Mrs Simpson.'

'But I'm still not sure how.' I stare at her without seeing. 'Besides, I don't have a clue how to go about it.'

'Maybe not, but that's where Nick comes in. We all think you'll be a natural – with your mum and stuff—'

'My mum!'

She winks at me and heads to the door. 'Let me know how it goes.'

The door swooshes shut behind her.

My big chance. I sit in class giving myself a pep talk. Part of me feels betrayed and ganged up on by my friends, but another part feels all giddy and stupidly excited. When lessons are over for the day, I mostly feel self-conscious and scared. But the main thing I need to focus on is helping Mrs Simpson stay in her own home.

I put on lip gloss, brush my hair, and go to the school library. I'm half expecting the other members of The Secret Cooking Club to be sitting at a nearby table, giggling and laughing. But other than a couple of older kids studying for their GCSEs, the library's empty.

I grab a random book from a random shelf and flip halfway through it before I realize that it's about the history of train travel in Britain. I slam it shut and put it back on the shelf. Then I have an idea. I ask the librarian if there's a cooking section. She raises an eyebrow like I've asked for something strange, and points me to a shelf at the back.

There are a couple of books for little kids – teddy bears' picnics and cooking around the world; plus a few of the usual Jamie Olivers and Delia Smiths. At the end of the shelf there's a tattered old book bound in blue leather that's turned around back to front. I take it off the shelf. It's a copy of *Recipes Passed Down from Mother to Daughter* that Mrs

Simpson has in her kitchen. I flip through the recipes, realizing that – because of Mrs Simpson's handmade, handwritten recipe book – I could cook any of them. Best of all, I'd no longer be scared to try. In fact, I *want* to try them all, and share Mrs Simpson's recipes with even more kids.

And that's exactly what I'm going to do.

29

THE PLAN IN ACTION

I'm going to start my own website. It's going to be called 'The Secret Cooking Club'. I'll put on lots of recipes and photos and inspire other kids to make things secretly for their school. There will be a page called 'Scrummy Cakes and Bakes', one called 'Home-cooked Dinners' and one called 'Recipes for Sharing'. And then I'll write about this really cool old lady who's helping us and about her special handwritten recipe book. I'll post photos of the book, the recipes, and all the little drawings and rhymes.

And when it's all up and running, I'll send the website link to Mr Kruffs. He'll see that we're online and if he tries to put Mrs Simpson in a home, he'll have no end of bad publicity.

'Hi, Scarlett.'

The dream dissolves like sugar in water.

'Oh – um – hi, Nick.'

'Sorry I'm late.' He plonks his bag down at the table. 'I've got to leave in thirty, so let's get started.'

'Great.' I walk over to the table and sit down beside him, trying to remember how to breathe. I let a curtain of hair fall over my eyes so that I can watch his every move. His hands are slender, his fingers graceful as he takes his laptop out of his bag and turns it on.

'So, were you thinking of a blog, or what?' he asks me.

'Yeah – a blog, plus a website where I can post some photos and people can leave comments,' I brainstorm aloud. 'Maybe a place for guest posts too.'

'So, kind of like your mum's?'

I shudder. I can't believe I'm doing this. 'Well, it won't *really* be like hers.'

'No, I guess not.'

My mind races to think of something to say as the computer boots up.

'My mum won't let me use the internet at home,' I ramble. 'So I don't really know much about it. But I thought I might like to learn.'

He turns to me. 'Are you trying to get back at her?'

'What do you mean?'

'Your mum,' he says. 'To be honest, I was kind of surprised when Ali told me you wanted to set up a website. I've always thought that you had it pretty rough, with your mum writing about you and everything.'

'You did?' My awkwardness begins to melt away.

'I remember a few years back – you used to always speak up in class. You knew all the answers and you had lots of ideas – you were really clever.'

I give him a wobbly smile. 'Really?'

'But then you stopped. After people found out about the blog.'

'Well . . . I guess . . .' I sigh. 'Yeah, that's probably true.'

He types in his password. 'I'm sure your mum is cool and all, but I know I'd hate it if anyone wrote like that about me on the internet.'

'She isn't cool. I hate that she does it. Most people don't understand.'

His smile makes me feel warm and tingly. 'Maybe more people understand than you think.'

I mull this over as he opens up a web page.

'So there are some pretty good blogging sites

out there. I think this one's the best.' He types something into the browser. 'It's called Bloggerific. It's pretty easy to post photos, text and video. And you can search by hashtags – so you can follow people, and people can find you.'

'Um . . . OK.'

'Here, I'll show you.'

For the next twenty minutes, I half watch what Nick does, and half understand it. The rest of the time I'm watching him, and enjoying sitting next to the scrummiest boy in our year who thinks I must be clever, and who 'understands' that I haven't had things exactly easy. I ask a few questions, but I can't bring myself to ask the BIG question – he and Alison hang out at school and she talks about him all the time – do they have a thing going? Or is there hope for someone like me?

'Scarlett?' I realize that Nick is waiting for a response from me.

'Oh, sorry. I was just trying to concentrate – it's a lot to take in.'

'Well, I'm sorry that I have to rush off. But let me know how you get on and if you need any more help.' He shuts down his computer. The electricity fizzles out of my body.

'Thank you so much,' I say. The words can't express my muddled-up feelings. 'I know you're busy, but I really appreciate your help.'

He hesitates for a second. 'Well, if you really want to thank me, there's something you can do for me too.'

'Oh, what's that?'

'Would you consider taking on a new member?'

30

THE FIRST POST

I'm fully prepared for my feet not to touch the ground. But actually, I'm remarkably calm as I leave the library. It's like the whole Nick Farr thing has made me grow up all in the course of a single day. I grip the paper with his phone number in my hand. I've agreed to contact him the next time The Secret Cooking Club meets – so that he can join us!

'For the record, Alison didn't tell me that you were the ones leaving the free samples,' he'd re-assured me after seeing my astonished face. 'I guessed that day I saw you out of class just before lunch. And I think it would be fun to learn a bit about cooking. I mean, lots of blokes do it these days. And Mum and Dad don't have time to cook – it would be nice if I could surprise them by cooking something good once in a while.'

'Yeah,' I'd said. 'I think it's something that anyone can enjoy doing. I mean, we all have to eat, don't we?'

He laughed. 'Yes, we do. Also, my mum has a big birthday coming up. Dad's planning a party for her and I'm supposed to order a cake. But how awesome would it be if I could actually make her one?'

'It sounds great,' I said. 'And we'd all be happy to pitch in.'

'OK,' he said. 'My rugby schedule's a little hectic right now, but I should be able to meet you one night next week? Monday?'

He'd written down his number and left for his practice. I'd rushed off to meet the other members at Mrs Simpson's house.

When I get there and let myself inside, everything is quiet, dark and empty. In the kitchen, I see that some work has been done to repaint the wall and fix the window. It looks as good as new. Obviously, Mr Kruffs didn't waste any time getting workmen in. And if he was here, then where is his aunt now? I'm sure that we'd arranged to meet her today. I was hoping she would be here so I could tell her about the new website – and about Nick wanting to join us.

I don't feel like going home so I nose around a little. Something is scribbled on the magnetic message pad that hangs on the fridge: 'Gone to visit a friend – RS.'

That explains where Mrs Simpson is, at least. It must have been a last-minute thing. Relieved, I sit down at the table and take a notebook and pen out of my school bag. The words pop into my head and I begin to write:

Please don't tell my mum that you're reading this. I mean, you probably won't because you don't know who I am, so you don't know who she is. And I don't know who you are. For now, I think we ought to keep it that way. It will be our secret.

You see, I have this problem with my mum. She's a blogger, and she's made my life a nightmare by posting lots of embarrassing stuff about me. I pretty much had to drop all my activities at school, it was getting so annoying.

I pause and read over what I've written, crossing out and changing a few words here and there.

But now I've started doing something that Mum doesn't know about. Don't worry, it's nothing bad. It's just that my neighbour was taken away in an ambulance, and when I went to feed her cat, I found this amazing kitchen and a special handwritten recipe book. And there was this new girl at school, and I told her about what I found, and she wanted to join me. So that's our secret – we're learning how to cook. Now there's five of us – four girls and one boy, plus the old lady whose kitchen we use. We're a real club – a secret club. No one knows who we are.

Except you . . .

And that's what this blog is about. We'd like you to join us. Leave a comment below, and welcome to 'The Secret Cooking Club'.

Yours truly,

The Little Cook

P.S. Don't tell any grown-ups!

I put down the pen. Luckily, I've read enough of Mum's blog to know how to do it. I think it sounds chatty, and says what I want to say. I've chosen to sign it as 'The Little Cook' in honour of Mrs Simpson's book. A strange feeling comes over me – not the calm of earlier, but more like the jolt of an electric shock. I was *meant* to come here and find the special recipe book. I'm *meant* to be doing this.

Just then, the front door opens. I jump up and pack my papers away. There's a loud screech and the sound of small feet running. Then, voices:

'Owwh, he scratched me!'

'Well, I guess he's just hungry, and glad to be home.'

'Achoo! I'm allergic to fur.'

Something small and black darts across the kitchen floor in front of me. 'Treacle!' I say happily. The cat goes next to the fridge where his bowl used to be and begins to meow indignantly.

'Hi, Scarlett.' Violet comes in with Treacle's bowl in her hand. She puts a finger to her lips. 'We were out kidnapping Treacle.'

'Kidnapping?'

'Well, cat-napping actually.' Gretchen giggles. Alison gives another big sneeze.

'Where was he?' I ask.

'At the cattery on Priory Road.' Violet sets down his bowl and I fill it with cat food. 'I asked my aunt to find out from Mr Kruffs where he had taken the cat. She told him that we were thinking of adopting him, but really we just wanted to surprise Mrs Simpson. Do you know where Mrs Simpson is?'

'She left a note – she's visiting a friend.'

'Oh,' Violet says. 'That's good – I guess. We came here earlier. The workmen were just leaving, but I was a little worried when she wasn't here.'

'Let's try to cook something, and maybe she'll be back in time for supper.'

The four of us start raiding the fridge and cupboards. Violet suggests that we try to make

'Simple Simon's Cottage Pie'.

I fetch the minced beef while Gretchen and Alison go out to the garden to pick some of the end-of-season vegetables. Violet chops the potatoes for the mash.

'Where were you, by the way?' Violet says. Her little smirk tells me that she knows exactly where I was.

My calm, cool resolve fades and I break out into a silly grin. It's all just too insane to think that I was setting up a website with Nick Farr and that he wants to join us. Gretchen and Alison come back inside. I suddenly feel self-conscious.

'So how did your meeting go?' Alison says, her eyes watering from the cat.

'Um, good, I think.'

'You think?' Gretchen jeers. 'Come on, Scarlett. You can do better than that.'

'Well, he's going to help me set up a website. An online Secret Cooking Club – I thought we'd have different pages: for 'Scrummy Cakes and Bakes', 'Home-cooked Dinners' and 'Recipes for Sharing'.

'What about something healthy too?' Alison suggests. 'Like "Healthy Bites for Home"? Mrs Simpson showed me a great recipe for fruit and nut protein bars. I'm dying to try them.'

'I like it!' I grin at Alison.

'OK, OK,' Violet says. 'Now stop avoiding the

real subject. How was it meeting . . . *him?*' she coaxes.

My face flushes crimson. 'It was fine. Actually, Nick wants to join us.'

'Join us?!' Gretchen and Violet say at the same time.

Alison shrugs. 'I guess he's a dark horse. He didn't say anything to me.'

'It will be really cool to have a boy member,' Violet says.

'Especially Nick Farr, right Scarlett?' Gretchen winks at me and blows a kiss.

'Very funny,' I sulk. *Is it that obvious that Nick makes me feel so strange – bubbly one minute and self-conscious the next?* 'But the more the merrier.'

'Maybe he'll invite the rest of the rugby team,' Violet says. 'They must eat a lot.'

'Maybe,' I say. 'But first we need to focus on helping Mrs Simpson. Here's what I have in mind . . .'

I outline my idea to the group. How we'll start a website, get lots of followers and friends, and raise money to help Mrs Simpson and other elderly people living alone.

'It might work.' Gretchen says. 'I mean, look at all the sponsors your mum has.'

'And like Alison suggested, we can have a bake-a-thon. But we'll do it online. We'll get sponsors and advertisers and pledges. And if we can get other kids to join us – kids from all over the place – they can bake things too.'

Alison beams – the bake-a-thon was her idea, after all. But it's Gretchen who takes up the brainstorming. 'It's a really good idea, Scarlett,' she says. 'And once we've got an online profile, if Mr Kruffs tries to force his aunt out of her home, we'll tell all his voters.'

'Do you really think it might work?' Violet says.

'Well, unless anyone has any better ideas,' Gretchen says, 'let's have a go.'

'OK, we will. And, there's just one other thing . . .' Taking a deep breath, I turn back to Alison. I can't believe the words are coming out of my mouth. 'I was just wondering – about Nick. Is he . . . um . . . your—'

Gretchen and Violet look at each other and laugh. Alison's perfect skin flushes a lovely shade of peach.

'No, silly,' Alison says. 'He's my cousin.'

MUM'S LITTLE HELPER

My mind bubbles like a boiling pot. The new website, Mr Kruffs, Mrs Simpson – where is she anyway? – and most distracting of all, the fact that Alison is NOT going out with Nick Farr. He's her cousin! No wonder she's so at ease around him.

We finish making the pies – they have fluffy mashed potato tops that are just browned, and the meat filling has lots of fresh vegetables, gravy and herbs in it. In the end, they are simple, but delicious. But for once, I can't finish mine. I pack the rest of it up in a plastic container, along with the one we made for Mrs Simpson. Despite the note she left, it's getting late and I'm starting to get worried.

We all pitch in to do the washing-up (double- and triple-checking that the oven and hob are turned off). Treacle curls up in his basket next to the range cooker. I stay behind after the others have left, hoping that Mrs Simpson might return. She doesn't. Eventually, I decide to go home. I lock the door and put the key back under the mat.

At home, I'm surprised to hear the TV on. It's way past Kelsie's bedtime, and Mum is always too busy to watch anything. But when I go into the front room, I see her – sprawled out on the sofa asleep, her laptop half tipped off her lap. At first I worry that she tried to wait up for me (luckily, both of us seem to have forgotten that, technically, I'm supposed to be grounded). Then I realize that she's just exhausted. For a second, I feel sorry for her.

I turn off the TV and watch her sleep for a minute, my brain ticking over with an idea. She won't allow me internet access at home, so I won't be able to upload my post or update my new website. But maybe there's something I can do to change that.

I move the laptop off her legs and she jerks awake. 'Scarlett?' She looks around her like she's in a strange place. Then she sees the laptop in my hand and reaches for it. 'Thanks for waking me,' she says. 'I've got some things to finish.'

'That's OK, Mum. I'm sorry you're so tired.'

'Well,' she shrugs, 'I guess that goes with the territory.'

'I was thinking . . . maybe I could help you. With some of your blog stuff. I could answer emails and post updates; maybe even respond to comments if you showed me how.'

Mum gives me a suspicious frown. 'You've never shown an interest before.'

'Well, we're learning about computer stuff at school. So I could use some practice.'

'Is this a new club you've joined?'

'No,' I say quickly. 'It's just that everyone else knows how to use computers and social media. I should learn it too.'

'You're probably right.' She purses her lips in thought. 'Social media is important. I guess maybe you are old enough to use it responsibly. But we'd need to set strict controls.' I can sense her blog-cogs whirring: *Help! My daughter wants to be online. Is this payback?* For once, I don't let it bother me.

'Of course, Mum,' I concede. 'And if I helped you, then you wouldn't have to work so hard all the time.'

'Hmm. I'll think about it.'

'I . . . um, could start now?'

'I'm too tired to show you right now.'

'OK, but once I've got a little practice, I'll be able to do loads. You'll need all your energy for your launch in Boots.'

'Well . . . I'll sleep on it.' She closes up the laptop and sets it on the coffee table. Her mouth gapes into a big yawn. 'Don't stay up too late.'

'OK, I won't.'

I haven't exactly got permission, but Mum's not one to turn down an offer of free help – even from me. We both go upstairs, and as soon as I hear her bedroom door shut and the water running in the bath, I creep back downstairs. I go to the lounge and open her laptop computer. It turns on immediately but it asks for a password.

Determined not to fall at the first hurdle, I go into the kitchen and try the door to the Mum Cave. It doesn't open. I push harder, thinking the door must be stuck, but it still doesn't open. It must be locked. I've never known Mum to lock it before.

I try the kitchen junk drawer to see if there's a spare key. As I'm rummaging through the bits of paper, old bills and yellow stickies, there's a loud thunk from behind the door to the Mum Cave. I go back over and put my ear to the door. Everything is quiet – I must have imagined it.

I look again for a key, but find instead a yellow sticky with the name and number of a computer repairman. On the back, Mum's scribbled her password: scarlettkelsie1. I'm surprised and even a little bit touched that she's used our names as her password. I return to the lounge and type it in. The screen flickers to life.

OK, I'm in – so now what? I pull up the Bloggerific website. From there, it takes me a confusing and slightly nerve-racking half hour to set up an account. I have to sign up for an email account on another site, verify my address, choose my template and figure out how to move around text boxes and photo layouts. Finally, I open a new text box, and slowly and carefully so that I don't make too many mistakes, I type in my first blog post as 'The Little Cook'.

When I'm finished typing, I look over what I've done. It's fine – I guess – but on-screen, it seems kind of dry and boring. I realize almost immediately what's missing. Mum always uses lots of cringeworthy pictures in her blog – irritating 1950s mums in aprons hoovering or doing laundry – with little sayings like: 'If only you'd do what I say, Mummy wouldn't have to LOSE HER RAG'; or making up not-so-funny little award badges for things like *Today I survived washing my daughter's gym kit*. All of her friends and followers always comment on how good they are. For my blog, I need some pictures too. Gretchen and Alison have both taken photos with their mobiles of some of the things we've made. That should do for a start.

I spend the next half hour trying to add some little empty boxes with the cursor where the photos will eventually go. But everything I've written ends up on the wrong lines or disappearing half off the page. Frustrated, I save what I've done as a draft and shut it down before I can make it any worse.

I'll just have to ask Nick. Poor me!

32

AN UNWANTED VISITOR

I leave early for school the next morning and go over to Mrs Simpson's house. Treacle is inside, meowing at the door, and there's no sign that Mrs Simpson has been home. My stomach knots with worry. Maybe she came home and Mr Kruffs had her 'old-lady-napped'. Or maybe she tried to get somewhere on her own and was hurt or injured. When we're cooking with her, she doesn't seem old and frail at all. But I remember the other times: in the hospital and the night of the fire . . .

Violet sees my face when I meet up with her in the corridor. Her smile fades to worry. 'She's not back yet?'

'No. What can we do?'

'I don't know – are you free after school?'

'Um, yeah.' I hesitate. 'But I've got a couple of questions for Nick – about the website.'

Her eyes light up in amusement. 'I bet you do.'

I give her a black look and walk off to class.

It takes me the whole morning to psych myself up to talk to Nick at lunchtime. When I approach his table across the canteen, the skin on the back of my neck prickles with goosebumps like everyone is looking at me and laughing. He's chatting with one of his rugby friends, but looks up as I come over to this table. I shift awkwardly from foot to foot.

'Hi,' I say, my voice croaky. 'Thanks for your help yesterday. I've uh . . . got a few follow-up questions.'

His friend raises an eyebrow across the table. My cheeks grow hot.

'Yeah, whatever.' Nick shrugs. I'm immediately sorry that I came up to him in front of his friend. 'I can't do today – maybe tomorrow?'

'Tomorrow?' I repeat dumbly. 'Yeah, that would be great.'

Before I can embarrass myself any further, I quickly turn and make a beeline for the girls' loos. I practically slam into Gretchen and Alison, who are standing at the sink painting their nails with rainbow stripes of pink and purple varnish.

Gretchen gives me a disdainful look for the benefit of another girl who's at the sink washing her hands. As soon as the girl leaves, Gretchen shrugs apologetically. 'Hi, Scarlett,' she says. 'What's up?'

'I need your photos for the website,' I say. 'All the stuff we've cooked.'

'I can upload the photos and help out with the website if you want,' Alison offers. 'You're going to need some help.' She gives a little smirk. 'Unless you and lover boy want to do it all yourselves.'

'No,' I say. I see in the mirror that I'm blushing. 'I can definitely use some help. Besides,' I lower my voice, 'we also need to find Mrs Simpson.'

'What?' Gretchen says, looking concerned.

'She's not back yet,' I say.

'And you have no idea where she is or who this "friend" is she went to visit?'

'None at all. It's like she's just vanished.'

We agree to meet at Mrs Simpson's house after school as usual. But everyone seems a bit preoccupied. It's not like Mrs Simpson was around at the start, but already she's become just as important as any of the other members. *More* important – considering that she's teaching us, and we're using her kitchen and special recipe book.

The house is still empty when we get there. Treacle meows plaintively like he's lonely – and maybe just a little unhappy with us for 'rescuing' him. Which he probably is. We find a recipe that we all agree on: 'Peter Piper's Pepper Pasta'. Gretchen and Alison go out to the garden to pick tomatoes while Violet and I mix up the fresh pasta dough. But my heart isn't in it. It takes ages before the pasta is ready to use: we have to roll the dough and cut the pasta, draping long strands around the kitchen. Gretchen and Alison have made a big bowl of salad and started stirring the spices into the sauce. It all smells delicious, and my stomach is rumbling. Now, if only Mrs Simpson would come back—

All of a sudden, there's a loud knocking on the front door.

'Aunt Rosemary – open up!' a voice calls out.

The four of us freeze, looking at each other in horror. It's Mr Kruffs. We've been caught red-handed!

'Aunt Rosemary – you know we need to talk. You're only making things worse for yourself by not taking my calls. I'm coming in.'

A key rattles in the lock. The door bangs open. Instantly, I'm roused into action.

I head him off at the kitchen door. 'Hello, Mr Kruffs,' I say, faking a pleasant smile. Violet comes up silently beside me.

'Where is she?' he says accusingly.

'She?' I give Violet a puzzled look. 'I thought the cat was a boy cat, didn't you?'

Violet giggles. 'I never looked.'

'Not the cat!' Mr Kruffs blusters. 'I'm looking for my aunt.'

'Oh.' I shrug dramatically. 'Sorry, haven't seen her today. She left a note – she's visiting a friend.'

'Friend? What friend?'

'She didn't say.'

He crosses his arms. 'And what, pray tell, are you doing here if she's not in?'

'Like I said the last time, I'm Mrs Simpson's neighbour,' I say. 'And her friend. We all are.' I'm relieved when Gretchen and Alison come up to the door behind me. Now it's four against one.

'You shouldn't be here,' he says. 'You're trespassing.'

I put my hands on my hips, feeling suddenly brave. 'So call the police. They might find it interesting that *you're* bullying an old lady – taking her cat away from her and trying to force her out of her own home. And even if they don't want to listen to us, I'm sure your voters might.'

Mr Kruffs takes a step forward. I grip Violet's hand and stand my ground. OMG.

'You don't know what you're talking about,' he

says. 'My aunt can't keep living here on her own. It's my responsibility to make arrangements for her.'

'What, so that you can sell her house and get the money for your campaign – is that it?' Violet says. I squeeze her hand gratefully.

He actually looks puzzled for a second, and then starts to laugh. 'Is that what you think? That's the craziest thing I've ever heard.'

'Well, I don't know.'

'No, you don't,' he says firmly. 'And we're done with this conversation. Go home.'

'OK, girls,' Gretchen says breezily. 'You heard the man. Let's go.'

'But what about the—'

Gretchen cuts me off with a raised hand. 'We'll just have to leave Mr Kruffs to do the washing-up.' Gretchen turns back to him. 'We were cooking supper. The kitchen's in a bit of a mess.' She smiles wryly. 'Could you make sure that the oven and hob are turned off when you go?'

'You were using the kitchen?'

'Of course,' I answer. 'Your aunt is teaching us how to cook. She's not here right now, but we have to practise. We can't let her down.'

'She's teaching you to cook—' He stops abruptly, looking genuinely startled.

'Yeah,' Alison chimes in. 'She's a great teacher –

the best. And she knows so much about cooking – she even wrote a special recipe book that we're using. The only thing wrong with her is that she's a little old, that's all.'

'Rosemary hasn't cooked in years. Not since Marianne died.'

'Marianne?' I say.

'Her daughter. But since you're such good "friends", I would have thought you knew that.'

To my Little Cook – may you find the secret ingredient. I swallow a lump in my throat. Mrs Simpson wrote the special recipe book for her daughter: Marianne. A daughter who died.

Mr Kruffs raises his hands in a gesture of futility. 'Aunt Rosemary heats up canned soup and barely eats that. A year ago she lost so much weight that she was wasting away. She had to be put on electrolytes and fibre.' He looks at me pointedly, like I should know what that is.

'Sounds awful,' I mutter.

'Yes,' he says. 'Not eating properly is one of the reasons she can't stay here by herself.'

'But her fridge is always full of food,' I protest. 'She has an amazing kitchen and all these cook-books. She *wrote* a cookbook by hand for her daughter. It's obviously her passion.'

Mr Kruffs laughs gruffly. 'And do you really think my aunt goes out to the shops and brings all the food back herself? Or do you believe there's a baking fairy that crawls out of her special cookbook at night and holes up in one of the cupboards?'

'No, of course not.' I don't tell him that actually, we've all wondered why the kitchen is always well stocked with food.

'Well, think about it. She doesn't drive, and the supermarket is too far away for her to walk there.'

'So . . .'

'So I have food delivered to her – or, at least, my PA takes care of it. Every week, like clockwork. And not just from the local supermarket, since I know how my aunt appreciates real food. It's from a gourmet market – they even put everything in the cupboards where it belongs, or out on the worktop, in case it might encourage her to try cooking something again. It's not cheap, believe me. But I don't want my aunt to starve, now do I?'

'No . . .' I admit, as I'm struck by a new possibility. What if Mr Kruffs is genuinely concerned for his aunt? We've only met her a few times – surely he must know lots of things we don't. What if before we met her she wasn't eating? And she did have a fall that put her in hospital . . .

'And now she's gone missing and you're here. She doesn't have any "friends" any more that live close by. So where is she?'

'I don't know,' I concede. 'And I can see why you're concerned.' I look at my friends. Everyone nods worriedly. 'But honestly your aunt seems OK. When we've been around her, she's seemed happy and she's eaten the stuff we've cooked for her. So maybe she's doing better than you think?'

He gives me a long look, and I can feel sweat beading up on my brow. I raise my chin and try to sound like a grown-up. 'Mr Kruffs, would you like to stay a bit longer and have some of the supper we've been cooking. It's just salad and pasta with home-made sauce – the recipe is from your aunt's special book.' I think of what Mum would say in her blog and take a deep breath. 'It might be a good idea if we all sit down and talk.'

33

THE WARNING

He stares at me. I stare back. The others look at me – surprise and shock on their faces. My heart bangs inside my chest.

'OK,' he says. 'Let's talk.'

What have I done?

Violet and Alison practically flatten each other in their hurry to set an extra place at the table. I'm amazingly relieved when Gretchen gestures for our 'guest' to take a chair and sits down opposite him. She sits up tall, looking every inch the cool, calm, collected PTA rep and future lawyer that all the grown-ups love.

Mr Kruffs crosses his arms, looking for a

moment like he's sorry he accepted the invite. I bring the huge wooden bowl of freshly tossed salad over to the table and sit down next to Gretchen.

'So, Mr Kruffs . . .' Gretchen is saying, 'how's the campaign going?'

'It's going just fine.' His eyes snag on me.

'That's what my dad says. You may know him – Alan Sandburg, QC.'

'He's your father?' Mr Kruffs straightens up in his chair.

'Yeah.' Gretchen smiles smugly. 'He says that you're a real champion of the "grey vote".'

'Of course,' Mr Kruffs says. 'Our elderly people are important members of society. We need to respect and value them.'

'And I suppose you'll have to travel up to London a lot if you're elected.'

'That's right. I'll be there most of the time. I've got a trip there planned for early next week.'

'Don't you have any family here?' I ask. Violet and Alison sit down and I pass Mr Kruffs the salad bowl.

He serves himself a generous plateful. 'I'm divorced,' he says. 'So, no. Other than Rosemary, of course.'

'It's so nice of you to care so much about your aunt,' Violet says. It sounds like she means it. I frown.

Mr Kruffs spoons on some oil and vinegar dressing and passes the salad bowl on to Alison. 'Whether you believe it or not, I do care about her. As I said, Aunt Rosemary is my only relative. Once she was almost like a mother to me. But her health has been getting worse lately. She's scattered and forgetful and sometimes she's unsteady on her feet. Of course she won't talk about it, but I think she may be suffering from dementia.'

'And what is that exactly?' Gretchen says.

'In simple terms, it means that she's losing her memory.' Mr Kruffs takes a bite of salad and chews thoughtfully. 'It happens to lots of old people. There's no cure, and she'll only get worse and worse. She might forget to turn off the hob, or she might forget to get dressed or feed the cat – or even eat regular meals. She's a danger to herself, and I can't always be around to look in on her – even if she wanted me to.'

We all eat our salad in silence. I mull over what he's just said.

'These tomatoes . . .' Mr Kruffs muses. 'I must say, they do taste very fresh.'

'Your aunt grows them in her garden,' Violet says. 'They're totally organic.'

'My aunt *grows* them?'

'Yeah.'

He narrows his eyes and finishes off his plate of salad. When he's finished, Alison jumps up and brings over the steaming bowl of spaghetti. It smells delicious, but I know I can't eat another bite. Not until I confess to what happened.

'Mr Kruffs, there's something you need to know,' I say, trying to keep my voice steady. 'Your aunt didn't leave the hob on that time it caught fire.' I grip the edge of the table. 'We did – accidentally. She was teaching us how to cook Eggs Benedict from her special recipe book. We forgot to turn off the gas and it was my fault that the tea towel caught fire. Not hers.'

Mr Kruff's face twists into a scowl. 'What did you say?'

'I said – we started that fire, not your aunt.'

He sits back, stunned. 'I could call the police right now. What you did was dangerous and stupid – not to mention a waste of public resources.'

'It was dangerous and stupid,' I admit. 'But . . . it was an accident. It won't happen again.'

I bite my tongue waiting for the explosion that I'm sure is coming. Will he jump up and push over the table, shattering everything on the floor? Will he really call the police, or drag us out himself?

So I'm surprised when he reaches for the bowl of pasta, and serves himself a heaping pile.

'Here's the sauce,' Gretchen says. Her hands are

shaking as she passes him the bowl.

He dips the ladle in the sauce, holds it up and looks closely at it, before gooping it over the pasta. Then he takes a bite, barely chewing it before diving in to take another. The rest of us watch in stunned silence – in a few seconds, he's demolished half the portion.

He sets down his fork and wipes his mouth with a napkin. 'It was brave of you to confess,' he says.

My friends and I all breathe at once.

'Not that it changes anything,' he says, serving himself more pasta. He passes the bowl to Gretchen, who takes a small portion for herself and hands it to Violet.

'It doesn't?' I croak.

'No.'

I swallow hard. 'But maybe Mrs Simpson doesn't really have dementia or whatever. If she's a little scattered sometimes, it might just be because she's old. And maybe she's sad about her daughter too.' *My Little Cook*. Gretchen gives me a sharp jab with her elbow. I ignore it. 'When did she die?' I say.

'Two years ago,' Mr Kruffs says. 'It was a car accident.'

Violet breathes in sharply.

'It was quick and painless – so they say, but she was Rosemary's only child. No parent should have to outlive their child.'

'Did Rosemary's daughter like to cook?' I ask.

'Like to?' He nods. 'She was amazing. She went to cooking school in Paris and Switzerland, and became a professional chef in London. The restaurant where she worked was awarded a Michelin star while she was there. I remember the Christmas dinners they used to cook together – it was like a banquet there was so much food. And all of it was perfect.' He smiles faintly. 'They were happy times.'

'It's just so tragic,' Alison wails, as she spoons sauce on to her pasta.

'Yes,' I say. The food comes round to me. 'But that doesn't mean that Mrs Simpson is crazy or losing her memory. Maybe she's just sad – or lonely – or bored. Maybe she just needs something else to do.'

Mr Kruffs shakes his head. 'As I say, her health is suffering. She needs to be looked after. And I can't do that. There are some very nice places out there with very nice people. Whatever you might have heard' – he snorts, sounding annoyed – 'and people say some idiotic things about homes for the elderly . . . well, there are a lot of good, kind places where older people are very happy. And safe. She'd make new friends too. It's just what she needs.'

'But we're her friends,' I say, feeling more and more upset. 'That's got to count for something?'

'"Friends" that practically burn down her house?' He glares at me. 'I think she can do without those, don't you?'

'It was an accident!'

'But it happened.'

I cross my arms. 'I know you're her nephew, but you can't just make her leave her home and go into one of *those* places.'

'Actually, I can.' His eyes glint coldly. 'I have her power of attorney, which means I can make decisions on her behalf. And I own a share of this house.'

'But it's cruel! She doesn't want to go—'

Gretchen elbows me even harder this time. I snap my mouth shut and stare sullenly down at my plate.

'I understand what you're saying about your aunt, Mr Kruffs, really I do.' Gretchen passes him back the bowl of pasta. 'My grandma was in poor health and needed care before she died. A carer came to visit her every day. And Dad installed a panic button in case something happened when the nurse wasn't there.'

Mr Kruffs fills his plate with seconds. 'I don't think that's going to be enough. In the last few months I've become convinced that she needs round-the-clock care.'

And then you can sell her house? I open my mouth

again but Gretchen cuts me off with a look.

'It's just something to think about.' Gretchen sounds like a real adult. 'An option.'

Mr Kruffs doesn't answer. He's back to eating the pasta like it's going out of style. I inhale the steam coming from my plate. Now that Gretchen's taken charge, I take a small bite. The fresh herbs and the spices of the sauce tingle on my tongue, the vegetables full of delicious flavour. The home-made pasta is silky and rich.

'This food . . .' Mr Kruffs says, wiping his mouth on a napkin, 'is delicious.'

'Oh, do you think so?' Violet smiles brightly. 'I'm so glad. Your aunt would be proud to hear you say so.'

He shakes his head in disbelief.

The bowls of pasta and sauce get passed around again, and the food is gone in a few minutes. 'Would you like some pudding?' Gretchen offers him.

'Unfortunately, I'm going to have to pass,' Mr Kruffs said. 'I must dash. The fact is, my aunt is still missing. I have to phone around and try to find her.'

'Has she done it before?' Violet asks.

He pauses before answering. 'A few times. Unfortunately, any old friends she has are scattered here and there. She's gone to complete strangers' houses before, looking for people she used to know who died years ago.'

'Oh.' I don't really have a good answer to that.

'Is it OK if we stay to do the washing-up?' Alison asks. 'We'll check to make sure that everything is turned off and we'll lock up.'

'You do that,' he says. 'But from now on, you need to find somewhere else to do your cooking – do you understand?'

'Yeah,' I say. The breath leaves my body like a punctured balloon.

'I'm leaving for London next week for a day or so,' he continues. 'Tuesday morning, early. If she's not back home by the weekend, I'm calling the police.'

'Fair enough,' Gretchen says.

I nod.

'Thanks for eating with us.' Violet cheerfully changes the subject. 'I think we all understand each other much better now.'

'It's been . . . interesting.' Mr Kruffs runs a hand through his dark hair. He nods curtly at us, and turns and walks out.

As soon as he's gone, the four of us open our mouths as if to talk at once, and yet no one speaks. Violet clears the plates from the table and Alison runs a sinkful of hot soapy water.

'What now?' I find my voice and turn to

Gretchen.

'You didn't help things by getting annoyed like that,' she scolds.

'And you sure were a Miss Goody-Two-Shoes sucking up to him like that—'

'I can't believe you told him about the fire!'

'Well, we can't let him keep believing that she did it, can we!'

'OK, OK,' Violet intervenes. 'That's enough. We need to think about what we do next.'

'We have to hope Mrs Simpson comes back,' Alison says. 'If he has to call the police, it will make things a lot worse for her.'

'Alison's right,' Gretchen says. 'There's not much we can do unless we find her.'

'But if she does come back, then how do we know we can trust *him*?' I say.

Gretchen smiles cryptically. 'Once she's back, I think Mr Kruffs will come around to our way of thinking.'

'What makes you so sure?' I snap. 'He seemed like a total creep to me.'

Gretchen rolls her eyes. 'Honestly, Scarlett. Don't you ever read your mum's blog? She's always saying that the way to a man's heart is through his stomach.'

34

HIDING OUT

I'm relieved when I get home that night: we've stood up to Mr Kruffs and given him more than just food for thought. Though I have to admit – Gretchen's grown-up way of dealing with him might have been more effective than mine. But there's still one big problem – where's Mrs Simpson?

For the second night in a row, Mum is working on her laptop in the lounge. Her hair is tangled and stringy, and she has dark circles under her eyes. But sitting on the table next to her is a lovely pink-iced butterfly cake, and the crumbs and wrapper of one already eaten.

'Hello, Mum,' I say, putting down my bag.

'Scarlett.' She smiles wearily and checks her watch. 'Let me guess – working hard on your science project?'

'Yeah, Mum, it's going to be really cool when we finish.'

'I'm glad you've made a new friend. What did you say her name was?'

'Violet.'

'Violet. That's pretty – like Scarlett.' She smiles.

'Yeah.' I start to head off.

'Sometimes I worry – that you don't have friends because . . .' She hesitates. 'Well, you know . . .'

I stop.

'. . . because of me,' she finishes in a whisper.

I stare at her in disbelief. 'Because of you?'

'I know – it was a silly thought.' She gives a little laugh. 'I mean, no one knows who I am for real, or who you are.'

'Um . . .'

'Except the people at Boots, of course. And maybe anyone who might recognize my profile picture. So really, I know it's not an issue. But you know . . .' she says, brightening further, 'I've had this idea lately. That I might move in a whole different direction.'

I'm not sure I like the sound of that. I press my

lips together. Now that I think about it, it's been a few weeks since she's written any 'bad' blog posts about me. After *The Single Mum's Guide to Dating*, she wrote a post for another site on *Best Mum-friendly Day Spas*, and this week's Friday post will be *Psst – I'm in Boots!* about her upcoming product launch. If that equals a new direction, then maybe I should be all for it.

'But anyway,' she shrugs, 'we'll see.'

'Sounds . . . interesting,' I manage.

'Would you like a cake?' She gestures to the plate. 'They're really nice. I had a big dinner and can't eat another bite.'

'Oh.' I peer closely at her. Mum's usual idea of dinner is a little tub of yoghurt and a bag of crisps – maybe a slice of cold pizza on the odd night. And certainly not fairy cakes. I recall what Gretchen said about Mum's blog and the way to a man's heart – maybe she's planning to start dating again. That would probably be a good thing – give her lots of stuff to blog about other than me.

'I'll have it later, Mum,' I say. 'And if you want to go to bed early, I can help you with your work – like we agreed the other night.'

She rummages through her papers. 'I've printed out some emails for you to update my contacts. Do you think you can do that?'

'Yeah, I can.'

'Well, then . . .' She stands up and flexes her fingers wearily. 'I'll leave you to it. And just remember – I'm trusting you not to be looking at any websites you shouldn't. Remember, I can always check.'

I give an offended shrug. 'Whatever, Mum. I'm just trying to help you. But if you'd rather I didn't—'

'No, Scarlett – I appreciate your help.' She walks to the door. 'As I say, I trust you.'

'Oh, Mum, one more thing.'

She turns back towards me. 'What?'

'Is something wrong with your office?'

'No,' she says a little too quickly. 'It's just that I can always smell cooking from the other side of the wall. It's really distracting.'

I eat the fairy cake and update Mum's contacts. When I'm finished, I go back to Bloggerific and log on. I'm not too worried that Mum might actually check up on me. Even if she sees that I accessed a cooking blog, what's the harm in that? I click on my draft blog post to update it. I manage to upload the pictures of our food creations that Alison emailed to me. The layout isn't quite right, but I'm satisfied that I've done the best I can. I hit the icon to publish my first post as The Little Cook.

The Secret Cooking Club Online is now officially 'live'.

I surf Bloggerific for a while, looking at other cooking blogs. I check back a few times to see if there's any sign that anyone has seen my blog. Of course no one has – it's only been up for minutes – what am I expecting? But then a little warning flashes on at the bottom of the screen: low battery. Mum doesn't have the charger in the lounge. It must be in the Mum Cave.

I set the laptop aside and go to the kitchen. I'm surprised to see loads of pots and pans on the draining board, all washed up and drying. Mum wasn't kidding when she said she had a big dinner. There are also three plates. Mum, Kelsie . . . and . . . ?

As unlikely as it may seem, I *know* who.

I go to the back of the kitchen and try the door to the Mum Cave. The door sticks, but this time it isn't locked. Taking a deep breath, I open the door. The room is completely dark. I don't turn on the light but whisper instead, 'It's OK, Mrs Simpson, don't be scared. It's just me, Scarlett.'

There's no answer at first, but a small circle of light goes on around the tattered old sofa that Mum crashes on sometimes. I blink at the brightness. A gnarled hand draws back from the light switch, pulling a faded quilt up to her neck. Her hair is a halo of silver; the lines in her skin softer and less pronounced.

'Scarlett,' Mrs Simpson says. She puts a finger to

her lips. 'You won't tell Emory I'm here, will you?'

'Of course not.' I step inside. Although I guessed the truth, I can still scarcely believe my eyes. I mean, *Mum* of all people is hiding our neighbour away – in her office?

'Your mother has been very kind,' Mrs Simpson says.

'That's good,' I say. 'Hard to believe, but good – really.'

'Won't you sit down?' She gestures to the swivel office chair that Mum got free from the tip.

I perch on the edge of the chair. 'We made you supper tonight and last night, but you weren't there. My friends brought your cat back too.'

She blinks. 'Treacle? Treacle's back?'

'Yeah,' I say. 'He's back. And your nephew came round.'

'Oh, Emory.' She sighs and tsks.

'He said some things, Mrs Simpson. Things that got me kind of worried.'

'What?' She grins toothily. 'That I'm losing my marbles and need to go to a nut farm?'

I blink in surprise at her language. 'Well, I don't think he's right or anything. But yeah . . . something like that.'

'What exactly did he say?'

I take a breath. 'He said that you weren't eating. That you forgot to do things because you had . . .'

'Dementia,' she finishes.

'So do you?' I ask, feeling scared of the response.

Mrs Simpson gives a sad little laugh. 'When you get to be my age, your mind is full of everything you've ever done in your life – not to mention regret at things you haven't done. With all that clutter, do you think there's room for things like what day it is and when it's time to go shopping or pay the bills?'

'Maybe not. But people still have to do those things.'

'Yes,' she nods, 'you're right, they do. But that doesn't mean they have to be shut away some place where people sit around watching television, eating mush, and waiting for a nurse to help them to the toilet, does it?'

I purse my lips. 'He also told us about your daughter. That she, um . . . passed away.'

She looks down at her gnarled fingers but doesn't answer. I press on, knowing that this is the key to everything.

'She was the one you wrote the inscription to, right? "To my Little Cook". You made the notebook for her. You cooked things together – you taught her. And then when she grew up, she went on to become a real chef. One of the best, Mr Kruffs said. You must have been so proud.'

A tear forms in the wrinkled corner of her eyes.

'Yes, you're right, Scarlett. Right about it all. Marianne was my daughter; my "Little Cook". She was everything to me. You also asked me once about the "secret ingredient". Well' – she takes a breath – 'it's something that everyone has to find for themselves – the thing that makes life worth living. My daughter was all that to me and more. And now . . . she's gone.'

'I'm so sorry.' I reach out and take her hand.

Her grip is surprisingly strong. 'Thank you, child.'

We sit like that for a few minutes without speaking. I wish I knew the right thing to say, but deep down, I know that there is no 'right thing'.

She draws a rasping breath. 'My nephew means well. And he's right about one thing – my health isn't what it once was. In truth, sometimes it feels like I'm marking time. I try to keep busy with the house and the cat and the garden. But as for cooking . . .' Her blue eyes are pools of tears. 'For a long time I couldn't face that. All those smells and tastes – all those memories.'

'I . . . I think I understand.'

'And then you girls came along. You broke into my home and shook up my life. You brought me those flapjacks in hospital . . .' She wrinkles her nose. 'Mind you, I was *not* a fan of the crystallized violets.'

'Oh!'

'But I knew then that my life wasn't quite over. I realized that I have things to do before . . .' She shakes her head. 'Anyway, I'm not going to let Emory put me away somewhere, even "for my own good", no matter how nice it is, and how much it might make my life easier. Not without a fight.'

'And we're going to help you.' I squeeze her hand.

'Yes, well.' She leans back on the pillow as if the effort is too much. For a second, she winces and rubs a spot on her head just behind her ear.

'Are you OK?' I say, suddenly worried.

'Fine. I get headaches sometimes, that's all.'

'Do you want a painkiller? I know where Mum keeps them.'

'No, child.'

We sit in silence for a few moments. 'We cooked him dinner,' I say haltingly. 'Mr Kruffs came round while we were making "Peter Piper Pepper Pasta" with salad and home-made sauce.'

She pulls her hand away, startled. 'You cooked for Emory?'

'Um . . . yeah. He came over while we were waiting for you. We thought feeding him might help.'

'And did it?'

'Well . . .' I hesitate. 'He didn't have us arrested when we admitted to starting the fire.'

She makes a move like she's going to struggle out of bed. 'You told him about causing the fire!' She claps a hand over her mouth.

'Yes,' I say quickly. 'I mean, we had to. It was the right thing to do.'

She sits back, stunned. 'The right thing . . . ?'

'Wasn't it?'

Mrs Simpson peers closely at me. I get the feeling she's seeing me in new way. 'Yes . . . if you put it like that. I suppose it was.'

'We couldn't let him keep thinking it was you when it wasn't! And I hoped . . . well . . . that it would be enough.'

'But it wasn't, was it?'

'Well – not really. But he did sound really worried about you. In fact' – I lower my voice – 'he said he'd call the police if you're not back home this weekend.'

'Pah! – the police! That's one thing he won't do. Not while he's in the middle of his campaign.'

'That's good,' I say. 'But maybe you can at least let him know you're OK?'

'Yes,' she says with a sigh. 'I'll do that. I'm a distraction that he doesn't need right now – I know that. And I don't want to be a burden to anyone.' Her breathing grows quick and shallow. A knot of anxiety tightens in my chest. She may not be off her rocker, but Mrs Simpson is really old.

'Don't worry, Mrs Simpson,' I say in a soothing voice. 'But is Emory really such a bad person? Gretchen didn't seem to think so.'

'No, he's not a bad person.' She sinks back into the pillows. 'In fact, he's a very good person. He and Marianne were practically best friends growing up. She loved cooking him his favourite puddings for his birthday and at Christmas – Emory was such a serious boy, but his face would just light up when he saw the food.' She smiles faintly. 'And when I put in the kitchen next door, he arranged everything. We were close once . . .' She sighs.

'I know the feeling,' I mutter.

'I know Emory just wants to do what's best. And in fact, he may well be right . . .'

'No, he isn't!' I say. 'Because we're going to look after you.' I take back her hand. 'Me and The Secret Cooking Club. And maybe' – I still can't quite believe it, but it must be true – 'Mum too. I mean, she let you come here and hide out.'

'Yes, she did.'

'And Gretchen knows about these things. You can get a panic button installed, with a pendant-thingy to call for help on if you need it, and have a carer come to visit you – even live in. You could go on like that for a long time. And if someday in the future, you want to go into a care home . . .' I shudder. 'Well, that should be your choice.'

'Thank you, child,' she says. 'I admire your spirit. And you've given me a lot to think about. It's good to know that even at my age there are still . . . possibilities.' She lies back in the bed, stifling a yawn. 'And now, if you don't mind, I think we both need to get some rest. It's been quite a day.'

'Goodnight,' I say, kissing her on the forehead. I give her hand a squeeze but she's already asleep.

35

FINDING THE MAGIC

The next morning I wake up late, exhausted after a night tossing and turning. I squint against the sunlight and the thoughts that are bombarding my head. What to do about Mrs Simpson? Can we make Mr Kruffs see reason? Has anyone seen my blog? And then I remember that I'm supposed to be meeting up with Nick Farr today after school. My insides go goopy.

I smell breakfast from the top of the stairs. My stomach rumbles violently. Mum is already in the kitchen with Kelsie. Mrs Simpson has cooked a huge breakfast of eggs, bacon and buttery croissants. Miraculously, my sister's plate is almost clean, and there's not a smear of ketchup in sight.

Mum beams at me as I come into the room. 'Scarlett, I see you've found out about my little secret.'

I stand there for a second, staring at her. Then I rush over. 'Thank you, Mum.' I give her a hug – the first one willingly given in a long time.

'Oh, Scarlett!' Mum squeezes me back. She smiles. 'And actually – it's no longer a secret. Rosemary called her nephew before breakfast and told him she was here.'

I step away, flooded with emotion. Mrs Simpson gets up from the table, straightens her apron and takes a plate off the rack for me.

'I can serve myself, Mrs Simpson,' I say. 'You eat. This is fabulous.'

'No, child,' she says. 'Sit down. This is my treat.'

It's like the kitchen is filled with a warm glow – food and kindness and unlikely friendships. Mum takes a second croissant and, closing her eyes, takes a bite.

'This is divine, Rosemary,' she says. 'I'd forgotten how good real food tastes. In fact' – she looks at me and smiles – 'I'd forgotten a lot of things that are important.'

I smile back, blinking to make sure I'm not still asleep and dreaming the whole thing. This can't be real.

'Tell her what you told me,' Mrs Simpson coaxes Mum. 'All of it.'

Mum takes a long breath. 'There are things about my past that I haven't told you, Scarlett. Things that were painful, and I wanted to forget them.'

I stare at her. Mum almost never talks about her past. Across the table, Mrs Simpson nods encouragingly like they've practised this.

'You may not know it, but my grandma used to live with us when I was a girl. She wasn't quite all there after her husband died, but she was kind and she helped look after me when my dad left, and Mum had to go to work.'

'Your dad left your mum?' I try to digest this new bit of information. I never knew either of Mum's parents – they both died before I was born. Dad's parents lived a long way away, so we never really saw them either. Because I never had grandparents, I never missed not having them. Or not knowing anything about them.

'My dad ran off with his secretary – I never saw him again.' She swallows hard. 'At first I blamed Mum – for losing my dad, and then for having to work. She was away just about every night. All she could find for work was a job as a barmaid pulling pints at a pub. I'd wait up sometimes until she came home, smelling of smoke, sweat and stale beer. I hated it.' She takes a long sip of the fresh brewed coffee.

'But when my grandma came to live with us, everything changed.' She stares off into the distance. 'It was like there was magic in the house. She was a wonderful cook, and she told stories, and she played the piano . . .' Mum drifts off. 'It wasn't magic really. It was just . . . nice.'

'It sounds like it,' I say encouragingly.

'Then she died.'

Mrs Simpson puts her hand on Mum's arm. 'Everyone does, my dear.' She gives a long sigh. 'But that doesn't mean the magic didn't exist. I know it existed when I was with my daughter, Marianne. It was an "everyday" kind of magic.'

'I don't know.' Mum's voice quavers. 'Not any more. I tried to shut it out of my mind for so long. I vowed that I wouldn't be like my mum – stuck in some degrading job, never having any money or any freedom.'

'Of course, dear,' Mrs Simpson says.

'So when your dad left, Scarlett – just like mine did – I was determined to take control of my life. I started the blog and that grew into something' – she hesitates – 'amazing. For the first time people were taking notice of me. For the first time, I was important.'

'No, Mum,' I say softly. 'You were important

before. To me and Kelsie.'

'I guess I should have realized that. Instead, I let the blog take over my life. I became just like my mum. Worse, in fact.' Her eyes glisten with tears as she looks at me. For the first time, I see understanding etched in the lines around her eyes. The things she did and how she made me feel. 'Much worse,' she says.

'Oh, Mum . . .' I realize that I'm crying too.

She takes my hand and squeezes it. 'But then I started to smell the cooking coming from Rosemary's Kitchen. It was like the memories were there on the other side of the wall, trying to find a way to creep through the cracks and crevices. All of a sudden, I was thinking about my mum, my grandma and my childhood.' She smiles like she's far away. 'And the strange thing was that it didn't seem painful any more. Just good. And . . . right.'

'I'm glad, Mum.'

She shakes her head. 'But I didn't want to face up to the way things were between us – and that it was my fault. And then the fire happened. I was so proud of you, Scarlett, and so ashamed of myself.' She sighs. 'And then Rosemary made that amazing breakfast . . . I went into my office to write about what happened. But instead, I shut down my computer and went next door.'

'You did?'

'She did,' Rosemary confirms, patting Mum's hand. 'We had a chat and a nice cup of tea.' She smiles wryly. 'Actually, a whole pot. She helped me clean up after the fire.'

'Really?'

Mum laughs. 'Honestly, Scarlett, even a toxic waste dump can get cleaned up if you put your mind to it. Which might be a good project for this weekend. We could tackle your room – together.'

'OK.' I smile warily. 'But you're not going to, you know, write about it? Or write about not writing about it?'

She sets her lips determinedly. 'I told you the blog was going to take a new direction. I've been thinking about it for a while – ever since the day you brought home those cinnamon scones.'

'Really?'

'Really. I've gone back and checked all the analytics, plus my comments and interactions. They all show a definite trend.'

'What?' I say, my stomach twisting.

'The bottom line is, there's a strong calling among my followers for me to become an "inspirational blogger".'

'A what?' I'm not sure I like the sound of that.

'I'm going to focus on *inspiring* other mums and women. I'll be kind of like an online coach for women who are looking to start a business, or change careers, or who just want a new lease on life. I want to help them to follow their dreams – just like I did.'

'Oh.' For a second I think she must be joking. But her face is serious.

'Which means, Scarlett, that I'm afraid you're no longer going to have a starring role.'

'I . . . I'm not?'

'No.' She smiles. 'I'm going to be a whole new mum to you and your sister. I promise.'

Something loosens inside my chest, and all of a sudden I feel a flood of relief mixed with another half-remembered feeling . . .

Hope.

'And Rosemary's going to help me,' Mum says. 'And we're going to help her – just like you did that night. After all – that's what neighbours do, isn't it?'

36

FRIENDS AND FOLLOWERS

I leave for school in a daze. It all seems like some kind of dream: Mum's story, her guilt, her 'new direction', and the fact that she's actually helping another human being who's in trouble. I don't believe in magic – not the fairy-tale kind, and certainly not 'everyday' magic, whatever that is. But I can't deny how much things have changed since Mrs Simpson came into our lives.

They talked about the details while I was finishing my breakfast. Mrs Simpson will get a part-time carer to look in on her, but Mum and I will help her out too. Mum will speak to Mr Kruffs and try to get everything squared with him. How she's going to find time to do all this, I'm not quite sure, but she actually gave me her old mobile phone so we can 'keep in touch' if Mrs Simpson needs anything. And even if Mum really is transformed, she and I still have a lot of issues to sort out. I accept that she's sorry, and I forgive her. But as they say, 'the proof is in the pudding'. Still, for now, it's much more than I ever expected.

The school day goes by quickly, and at the end of the day, my pulse goes into panic mode at the prospect of meeting Nick. I make my way to the library, worried that my knees might turn to jelly at any moment.

Nick is already there with his computer on.

'Hi, Scarlett.' He pushes his wavy brown hair back from his forehead.

'Hi.' I try to slow my breathing and sit down next to him.

'I see you've got your website up and running,' he says. 'I think it's a great idea.'

'Well, I did what you said. But I still need to sort out all the different pages, and I'm not sure that the layout is quite right—'

He beams at me and my heart almost stops. 'You've already got twelve followers. Not bad for less than a day, don't you think?'

'Twelve?' I lean over and scroll down the screen. The little counter at the bottom that Nick inserted shows that twenty-two people have visited my blog, and twelve of them have signed up to follow it.

'It's real, then.' My fingers on the keyboard begin to tingle with something like excitement. It crosses my mind that this is what Mum must feel every time she makes a new connection with a total stranger.

'Yeah,' Nick says. 'It is.' He helps me add the four additional pages: 'Scrummy Cakes and Bakes', 'Healthy Bites for Home', 'Home-cooked Dinners', and 'Recipes for Sharing' and add some boxes for uploading photos.

'Now,' he says, when all the pages are up, 'there are some things we can do to increase your following. Sign you up for some other social media sites and then link everything together. You've got to build your online presence – strike while the iron's hot.'

'OK.' I sit there watching him as he goes about setting things up for me. I know I ought to be paying more attention to the stuff he's doing, but instead I'm transfixed by his long fingers typing expertly on the keyboard, and his chocolate-brown eyes as he concentrates on clicking, linking, adding icons and creating my profile as 'The Little Cook' on other sites.

'What password do you want?' He turns to me, and I sit back, startled.

'Oh, um . . .' I think for a minute. 'How about "Buttercream".'

'"Buttercream" it is.' He types it in. 'Speaking of which, would you be OK for cooking on Monday after school?'

'Monday?'

'My mum's cake.' He flexes his fingers. 'I can't wait to get started on it. I can count on The Secret Cooking Club, can't I?'

'Of course.' I smile. 'After all, I owe you one.'

'Well, I'm happy to accept payment in baked goods.' He gives me a sly little wink.

'So it's true then – the way to a boy's heart is through his stomach . . . ?'

'Something like that.' He holds my gaze for a second.

My insides quietly melt. OMG.

THE SHOWDOWN

10 October: 9 p.m.

Thanks to everyone who's signed up to follow my new blog. I look forward to cooking lots of lovely things together.

Last time I told you about my neighbour – she had an accident and was taken to hospital. I went to her house to feed her cat and found a very old, very special hand-written recipe book dedicated to 'My Little Cook' – which turned out to be her daughter. So I thought, 'Why not give cooking a try?'

The first thing I made was cinnamon scones. They were so fluffy and spicy and delicious – you just HAVE to try them. Here's the recipe, by the way.

Oh, and be careful with the oven and the knife – you might need a grown-up to help.

Makes 14–16 scones

450g self-raising flour
Big pinch of salt
100g butter
50g caster sugar
1 teaspoon ground cinnamon
250ml milk

For the tops:
20g caster sugar mixed with ½ teaspoon ground cinnamon

Preheat the oven to 220°C/gas mark 7 and lightly butter a baking tray. Sift the flour and salt into a mixing bowl, add the butter and rub it in with your fingertips until the mixture looks like breadcrumbs. Stir in the sugar and cinnamon, then add the milk and stir the mixture together quickly using a round-ended knife. As soon as the mixture comes together into a soft dough, put it onto a lightly floured work surface and divide the dough in half. Try not to handle the dough any more than necessary. Lightly shape each half into a block shape, then very gently roll each half into a rectangle about 22cm long, 8cm wide and 2cm thick. Using a large chef's knife, cut each rectangle from one end to the other into triangles that measure about 6cm across the base. Transfer the triangles to the baking tray and sprinkle the sugar and cinnamon mixture generously over the tops. Put the tray into the hot oven, on a middle to high shelf, and bake for 10–12 minutes, until the scones are puffed up and turning golden on top. Place the tray on a wire rack to cool a little. You can eat them warm or leave them to cool completely, but they are best eaten on the same day. Nicest of all is to eat them warm, cut in half, spread with a little butter and then with any leftover cinnamon sugar sprinkled over the melted butter.

Oh, and definitely don't forget to preheat the oven. It works much better that way.

Thanks for reading this and I hope you enjoy making the scones. And maybe you can do what my friend and I did – we left them in the canteen at school without telling anybody who made them. Just say: 'Free samples from The Secret Cooking Club.'

Happy baking!

The Little Cook

When I'm finished writing, I upload one of Violet's photos of the scones we made. So far, blogging is kind of fun – not as fun as cooking, but I can see why Mum likes doing it. It's a way to connect with people – something that seems a little easier to do on the web than in real life.

As I look around my bedroom, I think about how much my life has changed since I started The Secret Cooking Club – not to mention a day ago when I sat in the library and actually flirted – FLIRTED! – with Nick Farr. And even though he had to leave to go to his rugby practice, knowing that I'll see him again makes all the good things seem real.

Monday afternoon, as I walk home from school, I'm still excited (and only a little nervous) at the prospect of Nick joining the club. I just know that we can make his mum an amazing birthday cake. But as I turn on to my road, my good feeling fizzles away. The black Mercedes is parked in front of Mrs Simpson's house – it's Mr Kruffs!

I quicken my pace towards the sound of loud voices that are coming through Mrs Simpson's open door.

'This is the last straw, Rosemary. I can't go on worrying like this.'

'But I rang you on Friday – you didn't have to come here and you don't have to worry about me.'

'But I do worry – you know that. I need to know that you're safe. Now get your things and come with me.'

'No, I won't. I'm not going anywhere.'

My heart jolts in my chest. Mum said she would take care of Mrs Simpson and deal with Mr Kruffs. Where is she?

Then I remember. She had a meeting with Boots today over the final packaging of her 'Mum's Survival Kit'. And now Mrs Simpson is all alone to face him!

I march up the steps to the house.

'It's for your own good, you know that! I'm just trying to help. Just come and have a look. It's a lovely place, I swear—'

'What's going on here?' I try to make my voice sound older.

Mrs Simpson is slumped on her sofa, her nephew pacing the room in front of her. Her face is a mask of defiance.

'You?' Mr Kruffs gives me a glare that could melt glass. But just then, I have an idea. I reach into my pocket and take out mum's old mobile phone. Before anyone even moves, I've snapped a photo.

'Yes, me.' I smile grimly. 'Scarlett.'

'What are you doing with that?' He nods at the phone in my hand.

'Just a picture that the "grey vote" might be interested in,' I say. 'Since you're acting for your aunt's *own good* like you said.'

Rosemary lifts her cane almost like a 'thumbs up' gesture. 'Scarlett,' she says. 'You always seem to be in the right place at the right time.'

'I try.' I grin at her.

Mr Kruffs checks his watch. 'This is ludicrous, Rosemary. You know I have to go to London tomorrow.'

'She's not stopping you,' I say, trying not to let my voice squeak with nerves.

'Stay out of this.' He waves his hand like I'm a pesky fly.

'But Emory . . .' Mrs Simpson's voice gains strength, 'I've been trying to tell you. You don't have to worry about me any more. I've found people to look after me. New friends. Scarlett and her mother.'

'Oh? Friends that set your kitchen on fire? And I don't see any mother – where is she then?' he says. 'When I came here just now, you were out wandering in the street. Why did your "new friends" let you do that?'

'I wasn't out wandering,' she protests. 'I was coming back from the corner shop. I needed more flour – we're baking a cake.'

'Baking a cake?' Mr Kruffs dark eyes look ready to pop. 'Since when do you cook again, Rosemary? I thought all that died with Marianne.'

She opens her mouth, then closes it again. Her lips begin to quiver.

'That's so cruel!' I blurt out, stepping forward.

'Talking about her daughter like that. That's just awful.'

'All right, all right.' He backs down. 'I shouldn't have said that. But *you* don't seem to have a clue why I'm here.'

'You're right,' I say. 'Mrs Simpson told you to go – so why *are* you still here?'

'Please stop, both of you,' Mrs Simpson says sternly. 'This isn't helping.'

Mr Kruffs and I both look at her, then at each other. In an instant, he pulls himself back into politician mode. I swallow hard, trying to think about how Gretchen would act.

'You seem to think I'm some kind of monster,' he says to me, his voice quieter, 'when really all I want to do is get my aunt somewhere safe. I called in a few favours and found her a place at a fantastic care home. It's only about fifteen minutes from here. She'll have her own room, with round-the-clock care. There are lots of social events, and even a kitchen where she could cook if she wants. This is her one chance – places like this don't crop up very often. I only want her to go over there this evening and have a quick look. If she likes it and then sells the house, she could be settled there for the rest of her life. She wouldn't have to worry about anything ever again.'

I breathe out slowly. 'She doesn't want to go.

She wants to stay here, in her own home. And we're going to look after her. Between Mum, and me and my friends, and maybe hiring a carer to help out – we can do it. And she's going to look after us too. Kind of like a grandma.'

Mrs Simpson hobbles forward and takes her nephew's arm. 'It's true, Emory,' she says. 'Catch your train tomorrow and don't worry about me. I'll ring you up and you can join us for dinner sometime later this week.'

He shakes his head in temporary defeat. 'All right, I'll go – for now. But I think you're all living in cloud cuckoo land.'

I step aside as he blusters out of the door and slams it behind him.

It takes me a second to realize that I'm shaking. I steady myself against the door frame. Rosemary sinks back on to the sofa like a tired, wounded animal. We look at each other.

'He's awful to you,' I gulp.

She closes her eyes and rubs her temples. 'He just wants to do the right thing,' she says. 'But I'm so tired of fighting. Maybe I should just—'

'No, Mrs Simpson, don't give up. You can't. It's too bad that Mum wasn't here. She would have sorted him out.'

'You did a pretty good job yourself.' She opens

her eyes. The fire seems to be relit in them.

'Thanks.' I smile. 'And don't you worry about a thing. I've got this.' I hold up the phone. 'Evidence that he's bullying you. He won't want that getting out.'

She squeezes my hand. 'Keep it if you like, but I don't think you'll need it. Now, where are those friends of yours?'

I check my watch. 'They should be here any minute,' I say. 'And by the way, that new member I told you about is going to be joining us tonight. His name is Nick. Are we still OK to help him make a cake for his mum?'

'By all means,' Mrs Simpson says, giving me a little wink. 'There's no reason why a boy shouldn't make a cake, or benefit from what else you're learning if he's interested. Though in my experience, we'd better start tripling the recipes . . .'

Right on cue there's a knock at the door. My heart lurches for a moment as I worry that maybe Mr Kruffs has come back. To my relief, I open the door and find that it's The Secret Cooking Club there in force: Violet, Gretchen and Alison – and standing behind them, Nick Farr. 'Hi, Scarlett,' he says. 'You OK?'

'Yeah,' I say, my cheeks turning crimson. 'I am now.'

38

HUNDREDS AND THOUSANDS

'Wow, this place is amazing,' Nick says, on entering Rosemary's Kitchen.

'Thank you, young man,' Mrs Simpson says. She smiles at him and then at me, a twinkle in her eye. 'Now, I understand that today we will be baking cakes.'

'Yeah,' Nick says. 'It's for my mum. She's turning forty.'

'A spring chicken,' Mrs Simpson says.

'Mum went to art college before she had kids. She used to be a painter. I'm thinking we could make a cake with lots of different coloured layers. Is that kind of thing possible?'

Mrs Simpson beams. 'I'm glad I bought two extra bags of flour if that's what you want.' She waves her cane. 'And if you want colour, try the bottom cupboard by the cooker. I'm sure this young lady' – she points her stick at Violet – 'will be happy to help you with the decorating.'

Smiling proudly at the compliment from our mentor, Violet goes to get the icing colours.

We mix, colour and bake, mix, colour and bake. Six layers in different flavours and rainbow colours; three separate cakes. A big cake for Nick's mum, a small cake for us, and a big rectangular rainbow cake for school. It's hard work, and even Nick the star rugby player is sweating before long. The first layers come out of the oven to cool, and Mrs Simpson oversees the decoration assembly line led by Violet and Alison. They've made three different kinds of icing – fondant, royal and butter-cream, and have filled at least a dozen different piping bags to decorate the cakes. Rosemary's Kitchen looks like a cross between an artist's studio and a swish London bakery. I take one set of cake tins to the sink to wash them out.

'Here, let me help with that,' Nick says.

'Sure,' I say, handing him a cake tin.

'I can't believe how much fun this is.' He picks up a sponge and cleans off the tin. 'It's kind of like science lab and my junior chemistry set all rolled into one.'

'It is fun,' I say. 'And I'm so glad you joined us.'

Just then, our sudsy fingers touch under the water and my whole body starts to tingle. Nick looks at me, and I blush. The moment is over, but it happened. Me, touching a boy's hand!

Two hours later, our special cakes are finally finished. We cut open our small cake, and everyone marvels at the rainbow layers in vivid colours. And more importantly, it tastes delicious.

Nick has brought his camera, and when we're done sampling our creations, he sets it on automatic timer. We all cluster behind the table around Mrs Simpson. The cakes look fantastic – white icing, decorated with rows and swirls of rainbow icing, glitter flower petals, and multi-coloured sprinkles called 'hundreds and thousands'.

'Smile!' Nick says. The camera flashes. We're all sticky and messy and happy, and there are sprinkles everywhere – hundreds and thousands.

'You girls – and boy – have a real flair for baking,' Mrs Simpson says. It's high praise coming from her, and we all look at each other and smile. The problems of the day seem long banished into the cloudy night outside.

'I'll be back tomorrow to collect the one for school,' I say.

'Are you selling it?' Mrs Simpson asks.

'No,' Violet says. 'We'll give it away. "Free samples from The Secret Cooking Club."' She smiles.

'You have a good heart,' Mrs Simpson says. 'All of you.'

'Thanks,' I say. At that moment I feel like I can do anything.

At home that night, I find Mum upstairs in her room. She's fast asleep, and while she's kicked off her shoes on to the floor, she's still dressed in a beige linen suit, slightly crumpled.

I kiss her forehead and she stirs in her sleep. 'Scarlett?' she murmurs.

'Yes, Mum, it's me.'

Her eyes open. 'I'm sorry I wasn't downstairs earlier. I was just so tired.'

'That's OK. I texted you that I was going to be late too.'

'Oh, I should have checked. I guess I'm not very good at being a mum.'

'It's OK, Mum.' I take her hand and give it a quick squeeze. 'How was your meeting with Boots?'

'Good, thanks for asking. They liked my ideas for the marketing campaign, and they're going to run with it.'

'Great, Mum.' I let go of her hand and turn

to leave.

'How's Rosemary? Did you see her?'

'Um, she's fine.' I go over to the bed and sit on it. 'But Mr Kruffs came over. He was really angry – a total bully. I tried to help Mrs Simpson stand up to him, but it was really hard.'

Mum props herself up on one elbow and pushes her hair from her face. 'I should have been here. Rosemary should have someone to watch over her. But . . .' She sighs. 'I don't even spend enough time with you and your sister. How can I look after Rosemary too?' She breathes out wearily. 'I had no business promising her anything really – it might mean I've only gone and made things worse.'

'We just need to find someone to look in on her every day. Like a nurse or a carer. Gretchen says that's what they did for her grandma.'

'But who's going to pay for that? Can Mrs Simpson afford it?'

'Well, she can pay some of it, I think. But I've thought of another way we might be able to help.'

I tell Mum my idea. She listens intently, her face lighting up.

'That's sounds like a really interesting idea, Scarlett.' She pauses for a moment, her brain ticking into blogging mode. 'I've got a few suggestions if you want to hear them . . .'

39

THE BAKE-A-THON

One month later . . .

15 November: 5 p.m.

I can't believe that The Secret Cooking Club Online has been up and running for a whole month already! Thanks so much to my 451 friends and followers – you are amazing – please keep writing in and sending photos of the lovely things you are making. And don't forget – when you leave free samples in your school canteen, leave a note with our web address.

Now for a few bits of news:

First, the countdown to the online bake-a-thon has begun. Only seven days to go! Click below to sign up and enter.

Second, I'm happy to announce that my mum – yes, you heard that right – is helping us in our push for 1000 followers. She's going to link my blog to hers and publicize us on Twitter, Facebook and Instagram. She thinks that together we can raise loads of money to help Mrs Simpson, and raise awareness so that other elderly people can get the care they need.

Third, we helped our newest member make the most AMAZING rainbow layer cake for his mum. She couldn't BELIEVE he could bake something that good. So go on, everybody, have a go – you might enjoy it!

I can't believe how much better things have got between Mum and me. I finally told her about The Secret Cooking Club, and also that I accidentally started a fire at our neighbour's house. She was surprised – to say the least – especially about the website. Things got a little tense again, but we got through it. And now it's almost like we're partners – and that seems to suit both of us down to the ground.

And you know what's surprised me most? It's that Mum can actually cook! For my birthday she made me a two-tiered cake with purple icing, strawberries and jelly babies on top – and it tasted really delicious. She and Rosemary sometimes spend hours in the kitchen, making real, healthy, home-cooked meals for me and my sister and my friends. And my friends and I do the same for her. We're finally learning how to respect each other.

And it feels good – really good. Maybe now that I'm thirteen, I'm finally growing up.

16 November: 8 p.m. Guest Blog by 'Shh . . . Mum's the Word'

I've never written a guest blog before on a 13-year-old's website, and all credit to my daughter for trusting me to do so when I've done little to earn that trust over the last three years. I want to say to 'The Little Cook' that I love you and am proud of you. But seriously . . . Help! My daughter's bake-a-thon is turning my kitchen into a tip!

17 November: 6 p.m. Guest Blog by 'The Little Cook' on 'Shh . . . Mum's the Word.'

You all know who I am – and way more about my life than I want. But now that I've found my own voice and Mum and I have talked through things, I feel a lot better about myself and Mum. I don't even mind her writing stuff (the good stuff, at least) about me – well, not too much anyway. But if you want the real story, check out my blog.

The best thing that has come out of all this is our neighbour – she's become almost like an adopted grandmother. We're trying really hard to raise money for people like her – elderly people living alone – so that they can all have a few more home comforts. And if possible, we want to help these older people get together to share yummy food and treats and make new friends. Click here for more information on our online bake-a-thon.

If you think this is a great cause, click on the donation link below and show your support.

Oh, and stay tuned for the bake-a-thon. If you're lucky, you'll have a member of The Secret Cooking Club near you to make something scrummy. We are dedicated to sharing happiness and friendship through baking. Even if you're (gasp!) a grown-up, we'd still be pleased to have you as a member. Here's that link again . . .

OK, so the blog is doing really well, and I'm enjoying 'meeting' so many new people and connecting with them. But as much as The Secret Cooking Club Online is proving to be a success, the bake-a-thon is keeping me awake at night. We're making tons and tons of food – not only for the school canteen, but for other schools, and for the hospital, and a few of the old people's homes in the area and for a couple of lunch clubs set up specially for older people. In other words, it's a big job. The good thing is that it's not just us – there are twelve people at our school who have 'joined up'. I don't know who they all are (because we have anonymous user names) but hardly a day goes by when there's not something delicious left in the canteen at lunchtime. Every day, I get from three to ten new followers on the blog.

Mrs Simpson is an interesting mix of grandmother, drill sergeant and kind fairy godmother. The one thing she insists on is that the blog doesn't get in the way of the main event – learning how to cook, and sharing what we cook, not just as pictures, but in real life with as many people as possible.

But not everything is going quite so well. For one thing, Mrs Simpson is getting a lot of headaches, and sometimes she loses her balance and seems to forget things. And Mr Kruffs is still in the picture, even though he seems to accept that Mrs Simpson is not going anywhere – for the moment, at least.

As soon as he got back from London, he turned up and paid another visit to Mrs Simpson. He came by her house and caught us with our hands in the cookie jar – or at least the cookie dough (Mrs Simpson was helping us to make chocolate-covered gingerbread people). And right away, you could tell that he wasn't too impressed.

He launched into his usual tirade – about how places at the 'nice home' don't come up very often, and wasn't Mrs Simpson tired of having to struggle through every day on her own? He also wasn't very happy when I told him that we hadn't had time to look into getting a carer yet for his aunt. But then the really bad thing happened.

Mum must have heard the commotion through the wall of the Mum Cave and she came over to add her opinion. She invited Mr Kruffs over to our house for a cup of tea and a chat about Mrs Simpson's future. And when I got home hours later and came into the kitchen, I couldn't believe it – he was still there!

'Hello, Scarlett,' Mum said, giving me a quick hug. 'Emory and I were having ever such a nice chat.'

'Oh?' I replied coolly. *Emory?* My eyes fixed on the half-empty bottle of red wine and the remains of a selection of nice cheeses that Mrs Simpson had bought Mum from a local shop.

'Yes,' Mr Kruffs stood up stiffly. 'Your mum is a very interesting person.'

'Yeah, she is.' I couldn't believe it. Is the "new Mum" all some kind of sick joke? Is she suddenly in cahoots with Mrs Simpson's enemy?

'Oh, not really.' Mum blushed. 'We were speaking about publicity, that's all. Building a profile and all that. Which I know one or two things about.'

'I confess that I'm not familiar with your mother's blog,' Mr Kruffs said. He smiled at her, looking almost boyish. 'But she says she'll forgive me.'

'Yes, of course.' She grinned back and their eyes locked together. Gross. 'Especially since I've started taking it in a whole new direction. Right, Scarlett?'

'Yeah.'

Mum's already started 'transitioning' her blog from nasty tell-all rant to 'inspirational women's blog'. For the 'parenting' section, she's had this new idea where she and I collaborate. It would be a 'dialogue' (her word) between a mother and daughter with a view to resolving their differences. At first I laughed and suggested that she'd have to come up with a whole new kit for Boots – *Mothers and Daughters Together* or some rubbish like that. Unfortunately, she loved that idea. I guess I'll try to keep an open mind.

'Anyway,' Mr Kruffs said to Mum, 'it's been very nice to meet you, Claire. I'll email you about that gallery opening I mentioned.'

Claire.

'Oh yes.' Mum's face looked rosy and flushed. 'Please do.'

OMG. All the blog stuff about 'The Single Mum's Guide to Dating' and the 'way to a man's heart is through is stomach' comes rushing back.

Mum is going on a date with Mr Kruffs!

'Excuse me,' I said in a choking voice. 'I've got homework.'

'Night, Scarlett.' Mum kissed me on the cheek. I went upstairs to my room and stared up at the glow-in-the-dark stars on the ceiling. At least they have stayed put while everything else is a whirlwind of change.

The day that I've been both eagerly awaiting and secretly dreading finally arrives. The day of the online bake-a-thon. Thanks to all of Mum's guest-blogging, tweeting and other publicity, I've got over eight hundred followers on my social media sites, and just over a quarter of them have signed up for the bake-a-thon. The format is this: everyone participating will bake something to take to their school, or hospital, or an old people's home, or local lunch club for the elderly, or just set up on the high street somewhere. Everyone is getting sponsors and publicity from local businesses. People donate to an online charity fund to help the elderly.

Of course all this is happening out in cyberspace and the world in general, so I have very little control over it. But so far, the donations have been coming in at a steady pace. I've had to set up a whole new site linked to my original Bloggerific account to accommodate all the photos that members have been sending in for each of our sections: 'Scrummy Cakes and Bakes', 'Healthy Bites at Home', 'Home-cooked Dinners', and 'Recipes for Sharing'. And as for my own branch of

The Secret Cooking Club – well, we've been cooking around the clock. Every spare fridge shelf, table, worktop, tin and cupboard is filled with the things we've made. And in a last-minute 'if you can't beat 'em, join 'em' move, Mr Kruffs called Mum and agreed to match whatever funds we raise from the bake-a-thon, in order to help pay for his aunt's carer. So now I'm even more fired up to raise as much money as we can.

I'm up and dressed well before the time that Gretchen's mum is supposed to come with her car to collect the food from Mrs Simpson's house. It's a crisp, bright autumn morning, and I can hear the birds singing in the garden as I go next door to get things ready. I let myself into Mrs Simpson's house quietly, in case she's still asleep upstairs. I'm surprised to find her sitting in her light-flooded kitchen, the doors to the garden flung open. On the table in front of her is a steaming cup of tea and one of the fluffy croissants that she helped us make. There's also a piece of paper and a pen. As soon as I enter, she folds the paper and tucks it away.

'Scarlett,' she says, reaching out her wrinkled hand. I take it and she grips my fingers. 'It's a lovely day for your bake-a-thon.'

I look closely at her lined face. Her cheeks have more colour in them than usual, and her eyes seem to sparkle, as clear and blue as the sky outside. She looks younger somehow. She's wearing her nicest flowered dress and ivory knitted cardigan, and her hair is smoothed back in a neat bun at the nape of her neck.

'You look nice, Mrs Simpson,' I say. 'Are you expecting company?'

'No, child.' She looks at me for a long moment. 'Not exactly. But there's magic in the air today. Do you feel it?'

I stand still for a moment – something I haven't done for a while. I listen to the sound of a pigeon cooing from the roof, the wind rustling through the orange and gold leaves. I feel the warmth of the pale sun on my face. Maybe those things are magic, I don't know. But I feel a little bit calmer and ready to face the day ahead.

'Yes, Mrs Simpson.'

She smiles. 'I'm so proud of you, Scarlett.'

'Thanks.' Her praise means the world to me. I lean over and give her a kiss on the cheek.

Just then, the doorbell rings. I go to answer it – it's Gretchen and Violet. 'Hi!' I say, ushering them in. 'Right on time.'

We go into the kitchen, but Mrs Simpson is no longer there – I see her outside in the garden, leaning on her stick and looking up at the sky. She gives us a little wave as we empty the fridge and fill Gretchen's mum's car with heaped baskets, pans and boxes of food. Alison and Nick are helping to coordinate food pick-ups from some of the new members at our school – Susan, Eloise and Fraser – who have made even more stuff.

Gretchen's mum drives us around to the places that we've pre-arranged – the hospital where we once took the flapjacks to Mrs Simpson, two old people's homes, the local council headquarters, a branch of a local charity that run lunches for the elderly, and several local businesses that have agreed to support us. We're left with a generous batch of chocolate chip cookies, brownies and cupcakes to take to school, and I have reason to believe that several more new members of The Secret Cooking Club (who we haven't met yet) will be bringing things too.

We carry everything inside through the back door of the canteen – everyone at school pretty much now knows or suspects who's a member of The Secret Cooking Club, and even if they don't, the dinner ladies are totally on board and helping us. They've even said that club members can use the school catering facilities (closely supervised, of course).

So by the time all of us pitch up to our first class (late), it seems that things are going well. I somehow manage to make it through the morning and all of a sudden, it's lunchtime.

As I leave the classroom, I can already hear the noise from down the hall in the canteen. Violet and I lock arms and go there together. As soon as I go through the door, I gasp. It's like a cooking flash mob. The tables are covered with baked goods – either The Secret Cooking Club has far more members at school than I know about, or else the dinner ladies had a go at cooking their own recipes and puddings. Everyone is standing around chatting and laughing, waving trays, not bothering to queue up in any orderly fashion. I'm happy to hear the clunk of coins in the 'pay what you want' collection box that we set up.

Then someone throws open the door that leads to the school lawn outside, and people begin filtering out for an impromptu autumn picnic. It's against school rules to do so, but the teachers don't try to stop us – they carry their plates full of food outside and sit down on the benches along with everyone else. Luckily, the day is still bright and sunny with a mostly blue sky and little puffy white clouds.

I grab a tray and edge forward into the clump of kids in front of the pudding table (I'm way too on edge to tackle any real food). Someone taps me on the shoulder and I turn round. Instantly, the butterflies take flight in my stomach – the way they always do whenever I'm around Nick Farr.

'This is fantastic, Scarlett,' he says. His smile is amazing, his eyes shiny.

'Thanks,' I say, blushing. 'Not that *I* had anything to do with it – but, I'm sure that *The Little Cook* appreciates your help with the website.'

'No problem.' He laughs. 'And I saw your mum's new post today promoting the bake-a-thon. She really has turned over a new leaf.'

'Well . . .' I roll my eyes. 'It's early days.'

'Listen . . .' He leans in closer and my heart practically stops. 'My brother and his wife got me two tickets to see One New Direction – you know, the tribute band? I was wondering . . .' His voice suddenly falters. 'I mean, if you're not too busy . . .'

'I'd love to go,' I practically gasp. 'When is it?'

'The Sunday after next. I can email you the details.'

'That would be great.'

All of a sudden I'm in the midst of the crowd up at the food table. I feel Nick take my hand and squeeze it, and then we get separated. I look around for him, my hand tingling, but he's gone.

I let the full implications of what just happened wash over me like a warm bath. *Nick Farr* asked me out to a concert. *Nick Farr* likes *me*!!!

The whole world feels like it's in slow motion around me. I grab a samosa, a fruit tart and a chocolate brownie, unaware of all the noise and the people pushing around me. I still feel like I'm flying as I take my plate outside and find Violet, Alison, and Gretchen sitting in a circle on a blanket on the grass. The others reach out their hands and we all slap high-fives. I sit down and take a bite of the fruit tart that Alison made – her speciality dish.

'Ummm. Delicious.' I close my eyes to savour the taste, and try to lock Nick's face into my mind.

When I open my eyes again, the sky is suddenly dark as a cloud passes over the sun. A few people look up and hold out their hands as the first raindrops start to fall.

40

THE SECRET INGREDIENT

By the end of the day, I'm exhausted but happy. I managed to sneak out of class for a toilet break at one point and checked our site on my mobile phone to see how the online bake-a-thon was doing. Hundreds of photographs had been uploaded, and nearly two dozen recipes. Best of all, we'd raised almost £3,000 so far for a charity that helps elderly people, and that's before anywhere near all of the pledges have been collected.

After school, I log on to the blog and officially declare the bake-a-thon a success. I can't wait to get back home and tell Mum and Mrs Simpson.

Violet stays to help me collect our dishes and baskets. Gretchen and the others go off to collect the dishes we left at other locations. But when Violet and I come out of the school building, I'm surprised to see Mum waiting at the loading zone in her blue Vauxhall Astra. We hadn't arranged for her to pick us up. Even though she's now a 'whole new mum', she wouldn't just have randomly decided to come and collect us. She leans out of the window to call to me, and it's then I notice that her cheeks are streaked with tears.

'Mum!' I cry. 'What's up? Are you OK? Is Kelsie OK?'

'Yes, yes, we're fine.' My sister is in the back of the car playing a Mickey Mouse game on Mum's iPhone. 'Get in the car,' Mum says. 'We need to go to the hospital.'

'Hospital?' Violet and I say at the same time. We look at each other, our faces stricken.

'What's happened?' I say to Mum. But in my heart, I've already guessed.

'It's Rosemary,' Mum says. 'Come on – get in.'

Violet and I shove our things in the boot and climb inside. Mum drives quickly. No one tries to talk over the squeaky voice of Mickey Mouse. As I stare out of the window at the traffic and people walking on the pavement, Violet reaches over and puts her arm around me. I bury my face in her hair.

We get to the hospital car park and find a space. I can't believe that just this morning we were here, worrying about our bake-a-thon of all things, and maybe even feeling a little smug that this time we weren't here to visit anyone. How quickly things change.

Mum half drags Kelsie along by the hand, and Violet and I follow behind. It takes me a second to register that Violet's got a basket of leftover baked goodies over her arm. We enter the lobby and Mum talks to the receptionist. She tells us to follow the yellow line – we're going to a different ward than last time. We go up in the lift and keep walking. The yellow line finally stops before a forbidding-looking door: *Intensive Care Unit*.

'But this can't be right,' Violet says. 'I mean, she was fine. She was . . .' Her voice trails off, helpless.

Mrs Simpson was sick. Really sick. And we hadn't even known it.

The set-up inside is nearly the same as the other ward we visited: the same busy nurses; the torturous-looking medical machines in the hallway; doorways to tomb-like rooms. There's an awful smell of disinfectant that doesn't quite hide the 'something else' underneath. I bite my lip to keep it from quivering.

Mum speaks to one of the nurses. The woman

barely looks up from her computer screen. 'Are you family?' she asks.

When Mum doesn't answer right away, I step forward. 'Yes,' I say. 'She's my grandma.' The words sound completely right.

The woman waves us to a bank of chairs across from the desk. 'Please take a seat,' she says. 'The consultant is on his way to speak to you.'

'But can't we see her?' Violet says.

The woman narrows her eyes like she's not used to argument.

'We'll wait,' Mum says.

We all take seats in the uncomfortable moulded plastic chairs. The room seems to swirl in front of my eyes. 'I . . . I don't understand,' I say.

Mum puts her hand on my arm. 'Rosemary collapsed just after lunch. She managed to press the panic button on that pendant we gave her. I went over right away and found her sprawled on the kitchen floor. She'd been picking herbs – mint, sage and rosemary – they were all around her. She was unconscious.' Mum's voice catches. 'Of course, I called an ambulance immediately.'

'Yeah . . .' What can I say?

She opens up her handbag and takes out a white envelope. 'And I found this on the table in her kitchen – right where she fell.' Mum's eyes glisten with tears. 'It's got your name on it.'

My hand trembles as I take the envelope. I stare down at the writing, the loopy letters of my name swimming before my eyes.

'She wrote you a letter,' Violet says. 'Open it.'

But I hesitate a second too long. A man in a white lab coat comes into the waiting area. He looks down at his clipboard, and then at Mum. 'Claire Cooper?' he says.

I shove the letter in the pocket of my jumper.

'Yes.' Mum stands up nervously. 'Kelsie, switch that thing off.' She reaches for the iPhone.

'You're Mrs Simpson's family?' the doctor asks.

'Yes.' This time Mum doesn't pause.

'Well, I'm sorry to have to tell you that the news isn't good. Mrs Simpson came in for some tests last week. She'd been having headaches and feeling weak, as I expect you knew. She knew that her condition was getting worse.'

'But she didn't tell us any of this,' I blurt out. 'I mean, I know she had some headaches, but doesn't everyone?'

The consultant nods. 'It was quite sudden as these things go. The blood pressure in her brain has been steadily rising. And today she had a major stroke.' He takes out a folder from under the top sheets of the clipboard. He shuffles a few papers, and then hands Mum a photograph. I peer over her shoulder. It's a grainy black and white scan of a skull.

'You can see the clot here – this dark mass.' The doctor points to a spot on the photo. 'And now she's slipped into a coma. I'm afraid that she's already beyond our reach.'

I look at him in disbelief. 'But, I don't understand. You mean she's . . . ?'

'Can we see her?' Mum asks.

'Of course, this way.'

My legs are unsteady as I stand up to follow the consultant. This time it's my turn to grip Violet's hand for dear life. Mum walks next to us, her jaw set grimly. Kelsie shrinks behind her.

As we begin heading down the hall, there's a pounding on the door to the ward and I hear a man's loud voice. 'Let me in, please. Someone let me in.'

The nurse at the desk looks annoyed as she buzzes the door. A whirlwind of a man in a black suit blusters inside.

'Emory,' Mum says in a choking voice. 'You're just in time. We're going in to see her.'

Seeing Mum seems to calm him a little. He comes over to her and kisses her on the cheek. 'I'm so glad you're here,' he says, ruffling Kelsie's hair. He glances at me and Violet. 'All of you.' The sadness in his eyes is genuine.

I look at the floor, unable to answer him. The doctor taps his foot impatiently. I lead the solemn procession behind him down the hall.

As we walk down the corridor, I force myself to look inside a few of the open doors to prepare myself for the worst. Just like last time, there are televisions blaring loudly, and wizened patients lying with tubes sticking out in all directions. I begin to feel dizzy as we walk.

The doctor leads us to a single room at the end of the corridor. I pause at the door and look inside. Mrs Simpson's frame is small and frail in the centre of the bed. Her skin is pale, her breathing even. She looks almost serene. The only tube coming from her is from a little finger cuff that leads to a quietly bleeping monitor.

At that moment, I lose it. I rush away from the room and a few metres back down the corridor, leaning against the wall and gasping for breath. The tears rise like a tidal wave inside me. The light blurs to dark in front of my eyes.

A hand grasps my arm to steady me. I blink and find that it's Emory Kruffs standing there.

'Scarlett . . .' he says quietly.

'You were right,' I say with a hiccuppy sob. 'She should have been in a home with nurses to look after her round the clock. I should have listened – persuaded her. If she'd gone to the nice home like you wanted her to, then maybe this wouldn't have happened.'

He gives me a kindly smile and shakes his head. 'No, Scarlett,' he says. 'I think *you* were right all along. She was old and ill – even I didn't know quite how ill – and this would have happened anyway. At least she was able to spend her last days where she wanted to be – at home. She was able to pass her gifts on to you and your friends – and that meant a lot to her.' His eyes fill with tears. 'I'm glad that, in the end, she stayed where she was, surrounded by her memories, and' – he squeezes my hand – 'by people she loved.'

I nod solemnly. In that moment, we seem to reach a kind of understanding. Maybe even a truce.

'Come on.' He gently tugs my arm. 'It's time to say goodbye.'

I allow myself to be led back down the hall and into the room. Violet and Mum are seated there on either side of Mrs Simpson, each holding one of her hands. Kelsie is standing behind Mum, her face almost hidden behind Mum's hair. Violet isn't crying, but her head is bowed. I recall how she was there with her mum at the . . . end.

She looks up when I enter. I can see the pain there in her purple-blue eyes. 'She's looks very peaceful,' Violet says, trying to smile. 'You know, like they say – on her way to a better place and all that.'

I shake my head. Wherever Mrs Simpson has gone, it can't be better than her lovely kitchen.

'I'm so sorry, Scarlett,' Mum says. And I can tell immediately that she means more than just about Mrs Simpson.

'No, Mum, it's OK.' My voice is remarkably steady. 'Um, do you mind if I sit with her for a minute with Violet?'

'Of course, go ahead. I'll be just outside.' Mum stands up and shifts places with me in the small room. As she ushers Kelsie out of the room, Emory Kruffs takes Mum's hand and they walk out together.

'Mrs Simpson,' I say in a whisper. 'Rosemary?'

There's no response other than the breathing. I grasp her wrinkled, arthritic hand. It's cool and slightly clammy. I look over at Violet. She's set the basket she brought with her on the spare visitors' chair.

I let go of Mrs Simpson's hand for a second and stand up. 'We brought you something.'

I go over to the basket and remove the cloth. I feel like Little Red Riding Hood, except this time I know full well that the wolf is already at the door.

'We've got scones, and a few flapjacks and chocolate-covered gingerbread people.' I smile through my tears. 'I know you like those.' I take the basket back to the bedside. I hold up one of the ginger biscuits under Mrs Simpson's nose. The delightful smell seems to fill the room as if they were just out of the oven. Cinnamon, sugar, golden syrup, spicy ginger. And something else is there too, underneath it all. I suddenly remember the letter that Mum found. I hand the cookie to Violet and fumble in my pocket.

I open the envelope and unfold the paper. It's only a few lines, written in Mrs Simpson's handwriting. I read it aloud in a soft voice:

My dear Scarlett,

I'm sorry if I didn't tell you just how short my time with you was going to be. But I thought it was probably better that way. I haven't known you very long, but I know that you already possess everything you need to become the young woman that you want to be.

The recipe book is yours, and I hope that you will keep it always and remember the times we had and all that we shared. Please don't be sad about me, but live your life to the fullest, and I'll be with you always. And as for the secret ingredient – you only have to look inside yourself to find it. And believe . . .

Love always,

Rosemary Simpson

Tears roll down my cheeks as I finish the last line. Violet begins to sob softly. And just behind me, I'm aware of three other people who have crowded into the room – Gretchen, Alison and Nick. It's only fitting that all The Secret Cooking Club should come here at the end, to say thank you to her for what she brought into our lives.

One by one, my friends all touch Mrs Simpson's hand – say goodbye, before going out of the room, leaving her in peace. Violet lingers at the door for a second before joining the others.

And then there's just me.

All of a sudden, I feel Mrs Simpson's hand underneath mine give a little jerk. Immediately I sit forward, hope flickering for an instant. Her eyes are still closed but her lips move slightly and a word comes out of her mouth: 'Marianne.'

Her hand grips mine more tightly for a second, and something like a smile plays over her lips. The heart rate monitor begins to drone a flat, steady tone.

She's gone.

41

EPILOGUE

The funeral of Rosemary Simpson is held on a grey Friday afternoon. In attendance is me, Mum, Emory Kruffs, my sister, Violet, Gretchen, Alison, Nick and about a hundred other members of The Secret Cooking Club who came from all around to meet up, celebrate the life of our mentor, and to bring loads of delicious food that would feed an army. The occasion draws such a crowd that the local newspaper sends a photographer, and the head of the charity for the elderly gives a speech praising our charity bake-a-thon. Many more people are present, not so much in spirit, as in cyberspace.

Mrs Simpson is buried underneath a shady tree in a corner of the graveyard, next to her daughter and her long-dead husband. I cry at the funeral – of course I do. But at the same time, I feel a strange sense of calm. I know that Mrs Simpson's with her daughter now – her 'Little Cook' – and that she's at peace. I know that the magic is real. And as for me – whatever happens, I can handle it.

I mean, I've already had to come to terms with the fact that Mum seems pretty serious with Emory Kruffs, and there's been talk of knocking our two houses into one (with Mrs Simpson's fabulous kitchen staying put, of course). Emory's actually OK, now that I'm getting to know him. Believe it or not, he and I have watched a couple of cooking shows together when he's over at our house. He told me a secret too – that when he has time, he might want me to teach him how to cook so he can make something special for Mum. So The Secret Cooking Club might be getting its first real 'celebrity' member – or, at least, our first MP.

But the one thing that does rattle me is when Nick Farr seeks me out after the service, offers his condolences . . . and then reminds me about our 'date' in two days' time to see the concert.

In other words, life goes on.

The evening after the funeral, I sit at my desk with Treacle curled up on my lap. At least so far, he seems content in his new home here with us. I finish typing in one of Mrs Simpson's special recipes, and close the little notebook. I press the button on my new computer to publish it on the blog – sharing what she left behind with all of our friends and followers. Beside me is a plate of deliciously fresh miniature butter pastries that Gretchen and Alison made, decorated by Violet with chocolate swirls and gold sparkles on top. I also have a steaming cup of hot chocolate topped with a sprinkling of cinnamon that Mum brought up to my room. I breathe in deeply, savouring the aromas and flavours.

A dash of friendship, a pinch of secrets, a cup of laughter and a dollop of tears.

And then there's the secret ingredient that's always there – something that we just have to find within ourselves.

Maybe you've guessed it already . . .

It's really not all that secret . . .

That's right . . .

Love.

ACKNOWLEDGEMENTS

This book is dedicated to Eve, Rose and Grace. I love you more than chocolate caramels. I'd like to thank the judges of the *Times*/Chicken House Children's Fiction Competition 2015 for choosing this book as the winner, and all the lovely people at Chicken House for making the dream a reality. I'd also like to thank my parents, my partner Ian, and my writing group: Lucy, Ronan, Chris, Francisco and Dave, for your support and belief. Finally, I'd like to say thank you to all my readers – you are the secret ingredient who truly bring a book to life!

TRY ANOTHER GREAT BOOK FROM CHICKEN HOUSE

DARA PALMER'S MAJOR DRAMA
by EMMA SHEVAH

Dara is a born actress, or so she thinks. But when she doesn't get any part in the school play, she begins to think it's because she doesn't look like the other girls in her class – she was adopted as a baby from Cambodia. So irrepressible Dara comes up with a plan, and is determined to change not just the school, but the whole world too.

'. . . a hugely entertaining read.'
ANDREA REECE, LOVEREADING4KIDS

Paperback, ISBN 978-1-910002-32-2, £6.99 • ebook, ISBN 978-1-910002-66-7, £6.99